THE
LIGHT
ON
HOGBACK
HILL

Other Avon Camelot Books by
Cynthia DeFelice

DEVIL'S BRIDGE
LOSTMAN'S RIVER
THE STRANGE NIGHT WRITING OF JESSAMINE COLTER
WEASEL

CYNTHIA DeFELICE, a former school media specialist, is now a professional storyteller, part of the Wild Washerwomen team, which appears at schools, libraries, workshops, and festivals. She and her husband have two children and live in Geneva, New York.

THE LIGHT ON HOGBACK HILL

CYNTHIA DeFELICE

AN AVON CAMELOT BOOK

For Shellie and Ralph, with love

AVON BOOKS
A division of
The Hearst Corporation
1350 Avenue of the Americas
New York, New York 10019

Copyright ©1993 by Cynthia C. DeFelice
Published by arrangement with Macmillan Publishing Company, Inc.
Library of Congress Catalog Card Number: 93-3507
ISBN: 0-380-72395-6
RL: 5.1

First Avon Camelot Printing: September 1995

CAMELOT TRADEMARK REG. U.S. PAT. OFF. AND IN OTHER COUNTRIES, MARCA REGISTRADA, HECHO EN U.S.A.

Printed in the U.S.A.

OPM 10 9 8 7 6 5 4 3 2

1 Hadley Patterson turned to see if someone was standing behind her, but there was no one there. Josh Carter, the new boy in the sixth grade at Possum Hollow School, must have been talking to *her*.

"What did you say?" she asked.

Josh's freckled face turned red, right to the roots of his reddish blond hair. "I said— Oh, forget it," he mumbled. He started to walk away.

Hadley, flustered, almost let him. But had he said what she thought he'd said? "Wait a second," Hadley called timidly after him across the playground. "Did you ask me if I wanted to come over after school?"

Josh turned back. "Yeah," he said carefully.

"That's what I thought, but I wasn't sure," said Hadley.

"But it's no big deal," Josh said quickly.

"Well," said Hadley, not sure now what to say, "did you mean it? Do you want me to come over?"

"Sure," answered Josh with a shrug.

"Okay," said Hadley.

"Really?" asked Josh. His face lost its careful look, and a smile curled the corners of his mouth. "Today?"

1

"Sure," said Hadley.

"Great!" said Josh. "But don't you have to call your mom and ask?"

Hadley laughed shortly and shook her head.

Three months before, Hadley's mother had been moved up from waitress to hostess at the Sheldrake Inn. The pay was a lot better, but Mrs. Patterson worked much longer hours than she'd ever worked as a waitress.

"My mom works late," Hadley explained.

"What about your dad?" asked Josh.

Hadley looked hard at Josh to see if he was making fun of her. Her father wasn't around, hadn't been since she was three years old. But Josh was new in town and maybe he didn't know that. Examining his face, she decided that he was merely being friendly.

"I don't have a dad," she said, trying to sound matter-of-fact. "I mean, I do, but he doesn't live around here."

"Oh," said Josh.

There was an awkward silence.

"Hey," Josh said, brightening, "if your mom won't be home until late, maybe you can stay for dinner. That is, if you can stand my little brother, Simon, and his dumb jokes."

Hadley smiled.

She liked the idea of staying for dinner. She was getting pretty tired of the instant macaroni-and-cheese suppers she'd been fixing herself, with an occasional chicken potpie or can of Chef Boyardee ravioli thrown in to break the monotony. Hadley's mother kept saying, "Next time I have a day off, I'm going to teach you how to cook some decent meals." But when the days off actually came, there were always too many other things to do. So they shopped quickly, piling the same blue-and-yellow boxes of macaroni and cheese, the same red cans of ravioli, and the same frozen chicken pies into their cart.

Hadley thought she could probably make something better. How hard could it be to open a cookbook and follow the directions? But she just couldn't get interested in doing all that work to make food that only one person was going to eat. Having a real meal at Josh's house sounded wonderful.

"I'll meet you outside Mrs. Dorsey's room after school," she offered, as the bell rang for the end of recess.

"Okay," said Josh.

Mrs. Dorsey was Josh's homeroom teacher. Hadley had Mr. Wolf, but everybody switched for reading and math, and she and Josh were both in Miss Cole's reading class.

Hadley was surprised that Josh had invited her over. She saw him only in reading class, so she didn't know him very well. She knew that he liked reading, as she did, and that he was pretty good at writing stories, especially mysteries. She knew that Josh's father was the new dentist in town, and that Josh's family had moved to town when old Dr. Hart retired. Hadley had gone to see Dr. Carter and found out she needed braces.

Josh seemed okay, and it would be fun to have somebody to play with after school for a change.

Hadley still missed her best friend, Alison Belker, who had moved away in the middle of the summer. Since school started, Hadley had become friendlier with some of the other girls in her class, but it wasn't the same as with Alison. The idea of spending the afternoon with Josh was a lot better than spending it alone, as Hadley had been expecting to do. "See you after school," she called to Josh as she hurried down the hall to her classroom.

2 When school let out, Hadley and Josh walked across the school yard, surrounded by groups of laughing, running, screaming children. Heading toward Josh's house, they walked behind a group of younger children who were carrying cutouts of jack-o'-lanterns, black cats, and witch hats. The children had made them in art class, Hadley knew, because she had made the same things when she'd been in first grade. Some of the kids were chanting in spooky voices, trying to scare the others, who listened, wide-eyed:

> "The horrible hag of Hogback Hill,
> If she doesn't get you, her black cats will. . . ."

Josh laughed. "What are those kids talking about?" he asked Hadley.

"Oh, nothing, really," answered Hadley. "Just the hag."

"Who's the hag?" asked Josh. "And where's Hogback Hill?"

"There," said Hadley, pointing ahead to a steep, rocky hill that loomed high above them on the other side of town. "But nobody ever goes up there."

5

The younger children kept singing:

"The horrible hag lives all alone,
Hump on her back and a heart of stone. . . ."

"Some kind of monster lives up there?" asked Josh, looking curiously toward the top of Hogback Hill.

Hadley raised her eyebrows and shrugged. "Depends who you ask," she said.

"She waits for a knock upon her door,
But those who knock are seen no more. . . ."

The children stopped chanting and, giggling nervously, they, too, looked at Hogback Hill.

"The hag of Hogback Hill?" repeated Josh. "Is this for real?"

"I take it you haven't met Angus Tull yet," replied Hadley.

"Who's Angus Tull?" asked Josh, looking confused.

"Angus is an old guy who lives here in town," explained Hadley. "He scares kids by telling us stories about the hag. He teaches little kids those rhymes, and they pass them around and scare each other to death. I used to have the worst nightmares because of him."

"But you don't believe his stories?" asked Josh.

Hadley didn't answer right away. She thought how, just the night before, she had lain in bed, hardly daring to breathe, staring out her window at the outline of Hogback Hill against the sky. How she had listened to the hooting of owls and the howling of coyotes and the sighing of the wind as it passed through the stunted branches of the trees that struggled to grow on the hill's steep, rocky slopes. How she had seen the light again, flickering at the very top.

Someone was up there; she was sure of it.

"I don't know," she answered honestly. "I mean, some of the stories are crazy. Angus says a hunchback lives up there, with a body all twisted and shriveled up, 'just like her heart.' He says she lives all alone except for hundreds of black cats, and that if you go up there she turns you into a cat and you're never seen again."

"Wow," said Josh. "Creepy. Well, the obvious question is: Did anybody ever actually get turned into a cat?"

Hadley could see that Josh was really interested, but she didn't want to talk about it. She had told Josh she *used* to have nightmares about Hogback Hill. The truth was that now that her mother worked late and she was alone in the house at night, the old bad dreams she'd had as a little kid had been coming back. The twisted shape of Hogback Hill filled her bedroom window, and the horrid image of a misshapen, witch-like woman filled her dreams. The woman reached out her arms to Hadley, beckoning with long, bony fingers. "Come," she called. "Come to me." And Hadley would awaken, tangled in the covers, her heart pounding, forehead sweaty, eyes staring into the darkness. She shuddered, remembering.

"Angus says his friend, Clarence Cuthbert, got turned into a cat," Hadley replied. "But I don't think it's true."

"But why would Angus make it up?" Josh asked.

Hadley shrugged. It was a good question. "I guess he just likes to scare kids."

"So you've never been up there?" asked Josh.

"No," replied Hadley, "but it's not because I'm afraid of being turned into a black cat."

"Then why don't you go?" Josh persisted.

"I—I don't know," answered Hadley. "None of the kids go there. Maybe you have to know Angus. He can really give you the willies." She paused, then decided to tell Josh the rest. "And, well, Hogback Hill is right behind my house. I can see it clearly from my bedroom window, probably better than anyone." She paused. "I think somebody *is* up there."

Josh lifted his eyebrows.

"Sometimes I see a light at the top." Josh's eyebrows lifted even higher, and Hadley went on. "It's got to be a lantern or a candle, because there's no electricity up there. And the light flickers. It's not steady like a flashlight."

"You mean you think somebody *lives* there?" asked Josh.

"I don't know," said Hadley. "But whenever it's clear enough, and dark enough, I see the light." She didn't tell Josh how frightened she felt when she saw it, how all of Angus Tull's stories suddenly seemed real.

"Why would anyone want to live up there all alone?" Josh wondered.

"I don't know," answered Hadley. "And even if someone did live up there, wouldn't she—or he—have to come down sometimes? And then everybody would

8

know who it was," said Hadley. She had thought about all this before, lying in her bed at night, unable to sleep, waiting for the sound of her mother's key in the door. It just didn't make sense. And yet, there was the light.

Her thoughts were interrupted by the tooting of a car horn. A blue station wagon pulled up alongside them, and a boy about five years old yelled out the window, "Hi, Josh! Is that your girlfriend?"

For the second time that day, Hadley watched Josh's freckled face turn bright red, right to the tips of his ears. She felt sorry for him. She blushed easily, too, and she hated it. Her hair was dark brown, not reddish like Josh's, but she had the same light, freckled skin that turned red at the drop of a hat. It wasn't fair to have a face that advertised your feelings to the whole world.

To make matters worse, Hadley had grown so much during the summer that she towered over all the boys in the sixth grade, including Josh. Of course, everyone in the sixth grade was taller than Josh. Hadley thought of how they must look, walking down the street together, the top of Josh's head not even reaching her shoulder. Josh's girlfriend? If she kept growing like this, she'd never be anybody's girlfriend.

Another voice called from the driver's seat. "Hop in, Josh."

"That's okay, Mom," said Josh. "We're almost home. We'll walk. Hadley's coming home with me, okay?"

"Certainly," said Mrs. Carter, smiling at Hadley. "Nice to meet you, Hadley."

"Nice to meet you, too," said Hadley.

"We'll see you in a few minutes then," said Mrs. Carter, pulling away from the curb.

Josh looked apologetically at Hadley. "Don't pay any attention to Simon," he said. "You know what little brothers are like."

"Not really," said Hadley. "I don't have any brothers or sisters."

"Lucky you," said Josh. "Well, here's my house. Enter at your own risk." He grinned.

3   "Why did the pizza cross the road?" demanded Simon as Josh and Hadley walked into the kitchen.

    "Oh, no, here he goes." Josh moaned. "He's on this riddle kick, except he doesn't really understand what a riddle is. He just asks a dumb question and gives an even dumber answer. Mom, make him stop, will you?"

  "I don't think Hadley would mind one little riddle," said Mrs. Carter. "Would you, Hadley?"

  "No," answered Hadley. She turned to Simon. "I don't know, Simon. To get to the other side?"

  "No!" cried Simon triumphantly. "It didn't know it was a pizza!"

  "See what I mean," said Josh. "Dumb!"

  "That's a good riddle," said Hadley. "Did you make it up?"

  Simon nodded. "You want to hear another one?"

  "No, thanks," said Josh. To Hadley he said, "Don't encourage him, or you'll be sorry, I guarantee it."

  Mrs. Carter was putting away groceries. "I'm so glad you could come over, Hadley. It hasn't been easy for

Josh, moving away from his old school and his pals and coming to Possum Hollow. I keep telling him it takes a while to make new friends, but here it is the end of October, and you're the first person who's been to visit. Of course, it's hard for Josh with his asthma. Sports seem to be so important to boys this age, and Josh has to be very careful."

"Mom!" Josh protested, embarrassed. "Make me sound like the dork of the world, why don't you?"

Hadley spoke quickly. "It does take time to get to know people around here."

Josh threw her a grateful look.

"I understand you and Josh are in the same reading class," said Mrs. Carter.

"Yes," said Hadley, surprised that Josh had talked about her to his mother. "Miss Cole's great."

"That's what Josh tells me," said Mrs. Carter.

"Not like Mrs. Dorsey," said Josh, making a face. Then, imitating his teacher, he said in a high-pitched, sorrowful voice, "And now, class, I want you to put your heads down and think for a moment about the way you've been behaving."

"Josh," said his mother, "that's no way to talk."

Hadley couldn't help laughing. "That's just how she sounds."

"You should hear her 'don't spin your books' lecture," Josh continued. "The first day of school, when she handed out our science and social studies books, she said, 'Now, children, don't ever let me see you spin your books.' We didn't know what she was talking about. So she put one of the books down flat on her desk, put her finger in the middle of it, and spun it around. 'Don't ever do this,' she said. I mean, we'd never even have *thought* of doing that. But now we do it all the time. It drives her crazy!"

"Josh," said his mother, "I hope you're not doing any such thing."

"Right, Mom," said Josh, grabbing two apples and a bag of corn chips from the counter. "We're going up to my room for a while. Oh, and is it okay if Hadley stays for dinner?"

"Is it all right with your mother?" Mrs. Carter asked Hadley. "Shall I call her?"

"It's okay; you don't have to call her," said Hadley. "Thank you."

"Well, we're glad to have you, Hadley."

Upstairs, Josh carefully locked the door to his room. "Anti-Simon device," he explained cheerfully.

"I think he's cute," said Hadley, munching a handful of corn chips. "Your mom's nice, too."

"Yeah," agreed Josh. "She's okay. She worries too much, though, about whether I have friends and stuff like that. She was really glad to see you, in case you couldn't tell."

"You're lucky," said Hadley. "My mom doesn't like me to have kids over. She says I can't have anybody over when she's not home, which is just about all the time, and when it's her day off and she is home, she says she needs some peace and quiet."

"Jeez, my mom's been driving me crazy, bugging me

13

to have somebody over. But, I don't know, it seems like everybody already has all the friends they want. Plus I have this stupid asthma, so I can't play soccer or football or anything."

"You acted pretty surprised when I said I'd come over today," said Hadley.

"I was," admitted Josh.

They ate for a moment in silence.

"So, anyway," Josh continued, "about Hogback Hill—do you really think there's somebody up there?"

"Some nights I'm sure of it," said Hadley.

"So when can I meet this Angus Tull and hear all his stories for myself?"

"Angus will talk to anyone who'll listen—about the hag, anyway. But I don't see why you'd want to meet him. He's weird. Scary."

"Well, if I'm going to live in Possum Hollow, I've got to know what's going on. I want to hear all about the hag—right from Angus himself!" declared Josh. "You want to go tomorrow?"

"Well . . ." said Hadley, stalling. She didn't really want to see Angus Tull, but she didn't want to disappoint Josh, either.

Simon's voice came from the hallway. "Open the door, Josh."

"Go away," said Josh.

"Mom says it's time to come down and set the table for dinner, so you have to open the door," insisted Simon.

"Okay," said Josh. "Come on, Hadley. My dad must be home."

On the way down the stairs, Simon whispered to Hadley, "What's gray and has four legs and a trunk?"

Hadley had heard that one before, but she pretended she hadn't. "I don't know," she said. "An elephant?"

"An elephant on vacation!" crowed Simon.

"Simon!" said Josh in exasperation. "It's a *mouse* on vacation. You mess up everything."

Hadley laughed, and that seemed to be all that mattered to Simon. He laughed, too, quite pleased with the effect of his joke.

Sitting at the dining-room table with the Carters made Hadley feel as if she were part of a TV family. Mrs. Carter was pretty and friendly, and Dr. Carter was handsome and full of good humor. They ate a meal that Hadley was sure would meet the approval of the school nurse, who was always talking about food groups and the importance of proper nutrition, and everyone sat at the table together, talking and laughing. At the moment, the topic of discussion was Halloween, which was two nights away.

"Dad, you're not going to dress up like a woman again, are you?" asked Josh.

"Well, of course," answered Dr. Carter.

Josh made a face at Hadley. "He does this every year."

"I thought dentists didn't like Halloween," said Hadley, "because of kids eating tons of candy and rotting their teeth and all."

"Not me," said Josh's father cheerfully.

"He hands out toothbrushes and sugarless gum," Josh told Hadley.

"You be sure and come over Halloween night," said Dr. Carter. "I don't want you to miss my new dress."

"And matching heels," added Mrs. Carter with a laugh.

Hadley smiled, imagining Josh's tall, skinny father walking in high heels.

"And I'm going to be a skeleton!" said Simon.

"Mom sewed the neatest costumes for us," Josh explained to Hadley. "They're made from black stretchy material, and the bones of the human body are sewn on the outside. They're made of this silvery stuff."

"Yeah," interrupted Simon, "but the best part is, in the dark they glow *green*!"

"What are you going to be, Hadley?" asked Dr. Carter.

"I don't know," answered Hadley. "Last year I made myself a pretty good wizard's costume. I'll probably wear that if it still fits."

"You can go trick-or-treating with us!" said Simon.

"Thanks," said Hadley.

After dinner Hadley and Josh helped with the dishes. Mrs. Carter said, "Hadley, why don't you come back for supper on Saturday night and bring your mother. I'd like to meet her."

"Oh, thank you," said Hadley, "but my mom will be working. Saturday night is her real late night. Sometimes she doesn't get home until one or two o'clock."

Mrs. Carter's eyes widened. "What do you do when she's at work? Does someone come to stay with you?"

"No," said Hadley. "I stay by myself. I'm okay."

Hadley could tell that Josh's mother wanted to ask more questions, and Hadley hoped she wouldn't. She didn't want Mrs. Carter to think she had a terrible mother or anything like that. "It's okay, really. I'm used to it," she said. "Well, I'd better be getting home now," she finished. "Thank you for dinner."

"You're very welcome," said Mrs. Carter. "And maybe you and your mother can come another time."

"Maybe," said Hadley.

Josh walked Hadley part of the way home.

"You go to sleep all alone in your house?" he asked curiously.

"Yeah," answered Hadley.

"Aren't you scared?"

For a moment, Hadley considered telling the truth. It was the kind of thing she'd have told Alison, who would have understood. But she didn't really know Josh. He might thing she was a baby.

"Not really," she lied. "I'm used to it."

"Wow," said Josh. Hadley could hear the admiration in his voice. "My mom still gets a baby-sitter for us. She treats me like a little kid."

Hadley didn't say anything.

"So tomorrow we'll go see Angus?" asked Josh.

"Are you sure you want to?" Hadley replied.

Josh nodded eagerly. "Don't you?"

Hadley shook her head. "Not really. I don't like him."

"Come on," urged Josh. "It'll be fun. An adventure!"

"Okay," agreed Hadley. She didn't want Josh to think she was scared. Not when he seemed so

17

impressed by her staying alone. And she wasn't scared—not exactly.

When they were halfway to Hadley's house, Josh said, "I'd better head back."

"Okay," said Hadley. "Thanks for dinner."

"See you tomorrow," said Josh.

"Bye."

While walking the rest of the way home, she thought about Angus Tull. She wasn't looking forward to seeing him again, but Josh had swept her along with his enthusiasm. And, she had to admit, it was kind of fun being the one who knew what was going on, filling in "the new kid." She liked the way Josh's face got all excited-looking when she told him about the hag of Hogback Hill. She liked his family, too. Even Simon, she thought, smiling to herself. She promised herself she'd go to the school library and look up some new riddles to teach Simon the next time she saw him.

4 As Hadley let herself into the house with the key she wore around her neck, the first thing she noticed was how quiet it was. Coming from Josh's house, where there was so much talk and laughter, her house seemed more empty than usual.

She didn't have any homework, so she switched on the television. She watched a few minutes of a show that was supposed to be about a typical family, but the parents acted like idiots and the kids talked back to them all the time. "Dumb," she said out loud. She turned it off. It was pretty late. She decided to get ready for bed and read for a while.

She checked the front and back doors to make sure they were locked, washed her face and brushed her teeth, and got into bed with her book. It was a good book, but tonight she couldn't concentrate on it. She kept thinking about Josh and his family. She thought, not for the first time, that despite what Josh said, it would be nice to have a little brother or sister. She didn't think Josh minded Simon as much as he said he did. If I had a little brother, Hadley reasoned, Mom would have to be home more, like she was when I was little.

When Mrs. Patterson had taken the hostess job at the Sheldrake, she had said, "You're old enough now to be on your own more and, goodness knows, we can use the money. You'll be okay in the evenings until I get home, won't you, honey?" And Hadley had said yes, she'd be fine.

What could she tell her mother now—that she wasn't fine, that maybe she wasn't old enough to be on her own? Besides, her mother liked her new job. It was much easier than waitressing, she said, and people treated her with more respect. And they did need the money. Braces, for example, cost a lot, Hadley knew that. She didn't want crooked teeth the rest of her life, did she?

So she didn't say anything to her mother about the long, dark nights when she lay in her bed, stiffening at every sound, watching the strange shadows that moved on her bedroom wall. She didn't tell her mother how much she missed the evenings they used to spend together after work and school, when Mrs. Patterson propped her tired feet on the coffee table and Hadley read out loud.

She didn't say anything about how awful the weekends were. Saturday was a big day at the Sheldrake, and they needed Hadley's mother to keep the customers flowing happily through the restaurant, and of course there was Sunday brunch. Mrs. Patterson's days off came more and more often during the week, when

Hadley was at school, and since Mrs. Patterson worried about Hadley having friends over when she wasn't home, the weekends dragged endlessly. It wouldn't be so bad if Alison were still around. But Alison had left—at just about the same time that Hadley's mother had taken the new job.

The nights were the worst. Many nights Hadley didn't sleep at all, waiting for her mother to come home. Like tonight. Hadley stared out the window. The moon was close to being full and, in its light, she saw the dark outline of Hogback Hill against the sky. She sat up suddenly as, once again, a faint light flickered near the top of the hill.

She got out of bed and stood at the window, looking up. She had the sudden, peculiar feeling that whoever was there was looking down at that very moment, watching her as she stood at her bedroom window. A shiver ran down her spine. "Who are you?" she wondered, and was surprised to hear herself speaking out loud. "And what are you doing, all by yourself, on Hogback Hill?"

Her only answer was the light as it gave one last flicker and went out.

5 The next morning, Hadley crept into her mother's bedroom. Mrs. Patterson was lying across the bed, sleeping deeply. She hadn't even gotten into her nightgown, but had fallen into bed in her slip. She looked exhausted. Hadley was supposed to wake her mother so that they could have breakfast together. But she knew her mother had come in after midnight the night before. Mrs. Patterson didn't have to be at work until noon. Why disturb her? Quietly, Hadley ate breakfast, got dressed, and slipped out the door.

During reading class, Josh slipped Hadley a note. It said, "Meet me by the swings after school. Don't tell anyone where we're going! Josh." Hadley turned around to see Josh's eager, excited face grinning at her. She grinned back. It was fun, the way Josh was making such a big, daring expedition out of going to see Angus Tull.

When school let out, Hadley found Josh waiting for her, full of ideas and plans. "Now, this guy Angus lives alone, right?"

Hadley nodded.

"And nobody knows we're going there, right?"

Hadley nodded again.

"So," said Josh proudly, "I left a note in my desk telling the date and our destination. That way, if something happens to us, like if this Angus Tull decides to murder us or something, there will be some clues left behind for the police to follow."

"Josh, you're nuts," said Hadley nervously. "Nobody's going to murder us. What are you talking about?"

"Hadley, you're the one who didn't want to go see this guy cause he's so weird. I'm just trying to take proper precautions. That's what you do when you're tracking down a mystery. Now, did you or did you not say Angus is a creep?"

"Yes, but I didn't say he was a murderer."

"Okay, okay. I'm just trying to get in the right mood here. I mean, tomorrow's Halloween, and we're going to the house of a nutty old man, tracking down the story of a hag who turns people into black cats. It's perfect!"

"Perfect," agreed Hadley sarcastically. "I can't believe you talked me into this."

"Let's go before you chicken out," said Josh.

"I'm not chickening out!" said Hadley.

"Then let's go," said Josh. "Lead the way."

"Angus lives on the other side of town," said Hadley, "sort of near me."

"Near Hogback Hill," added Josh in a mysterious voice.

"Yeah," said Hadley.

"What are we going to do, just go up and knock on his door?" asked Josh.

"I guess so," answered Hadley. "I've never done this before. Usually people try to avoid Angus. They don't go looking for him."

"He'll be surprised, then?" asked Josh.

"Probably," said Hadley.

"We don't want him to get suspicious," mused Josh.

"Suspicious about what?" asked Hadley.

"About us going up Hogback Hill, of course," answered Josh.

"Josh!" said Hadley, stopping dead. "I said I'd take you to see Angus. I never said anything about going up Hogback Hill."

"Okay, okay," said Josh soothingly. "One thing at a time. First we go to see Angus."

"We go to see Angus, and that's it," said Hadley, with what she hoped sounded like the last word on the subject. "There, that's his house. The one with the unmowed grass."

"Wow," Josh said softly. "It even looks like a haunted house."

Hadley hadn't paid any attention to Angus's house for a long time. She didn't have to walk past it, since it was the last house on the street that ended at the foot of Hogback Hill. But now, looking at it through Josh's eyes, she could see that he was right. The house had a run-down, uncared-for look, as if no one lived there at all. Untrimmed bushes and shrubs grew over the filthy windows, and vines climbed over the porch, almost covering an old rocking chair that sat on the uneven wooden planks. The stairs were crooked, with one missing. The house looked dark and empty. She could certainly see how Josh would think it looked like a haunted house.

"The place looks deserted. He still lives here, doesn't he?" whispered Josh.

"As far as I know," Hadley whispered back. She tried to remember the last time she had seen Angus. She didn't know when it had been, but she could picture him, walking down the street toward her, carrying a bag of groceries under each arm.

"What do you think we should do?" Josh was whispering again.

"I don't know," answered Hadley. As they approached Angus's house, the sun disappeared behind a cloud, making the late autumn afternoon dark and suddenly chilly. That, together with all the whispering, was making her nervous. "Knock on the door, I guess," she said loudly.

"Shhhhhh," said Josh, his fingers to his lips.

"Josh, you're getting me spooked. Why should we be quiet? When we knock on the door, he'll know we're here. I mean, you do want to talk to him, right? Wasn't that the idea?"

"Yeah," said Josh. "Okay, are you ready? Let's go."

They climbed the crooked stairs, avoiding the missing step. Josh pointed to an ancient brass door knocker in the shape of a winged lion. He was lifting the lion's head to knock when a black cat streaked out of the bushes and ran across the porch by their feet. Hadley screamed, and Josh dropped the heavy knocker with a loud clang.

Hadley held her hand over her mouth. She felt like a fool for screaming. Josh looked at her, wide-eyed "Black cat!" he said, grinning. "Wonder who that used to be?"

Hadley giggled. "Josh, don't be dumb."

All at once they heard slow, heavy footsteps approaching from inside the house. The curtain on the door was pulled aside, and they caught a glimpse of a frowning face, eyes squinting from under bristly white eyebrows. The eyes, a startling blue, stared at them for a long moment. Then the curtain fell back into place and the door opened. Angus Tull stood before them, scowling fiercely.

"Well?" he asked flatly.

Hadley wished that she and Josh had thought more about what they were going to say. She supposed she had to speak first since, although she didn't think Angus knew who she was, Josh was a total stranger. Her heart was hammering in her chest, and she could feel the blush starting to creep up her neck to her face. Josh didn't seem inclined to speak, so she began. "Mr. Tull?"

"Who'd you expect? I live here, don't I?" he said abruptly.

"Yes, sir. Uh, that's why we came. I'm Hadley Patterson, and this is my friend, Josh Carter. He—"

"He the one who tried to knock my door down?" asked Angus.

"Yes," answered Hadley, "I mean, no. I mean, he didn't mean to—"

"It just kind of slipped," Josh explained quickly.

Angus snorted. That appeared to be all he was going to say, so Hadley continued. "Well, sir, Josh is new in town, and I was telling him about, well, about the hag of Hogback Hill, and—"

"What about her?" Angus interrupted again. The mention of the hag seemed to have aroused his full attention.

"Just about what you say—that she turns people into cats and all," Hadley stumbled on, never knowing when Angus was going to jump into the conversation.

"You stay away from there, or the same thing will happen to you," Angus said suddenly, turning for the first time to Josh and giving him a penetrating stare.

"It will?" asked Josh, startled into speaking.

"You don't believe me?" snapped Angus. "Stupid boy. Clarence Cuthbert didn't believe me, either, and look what happened to him."

"What happened?" asked Josh. His bravado seemed to have disappeared, Hadley noticed. He looked the way she felt around Angus—nervous and scared. Well, this was what Josh had come to find out. Hadley had no doubt he'd hear the whole story now.

"In here," said Angus, stepping away from the door and disappearing into the house.

Josh and Hadley looked at each other.

"Does he want us to go in there?" asked Josh.

"Looks like it," said Hadley.

"My mother would kill me if she thought I went into a strange house like this," Josh whispered.

"Mine, too," answered Hadley. "Come on, let's get out of here." She grabbed Josh's hand.

"We can't just walk away," said Josh.

"Come on," urged Hadley. "Why not?"

"It would be rude," answered Josh.

"Rude! What about him?" said Hadley. "Come on, let's leave. I don't want to go in there. I'll tell you the whole story myself later."

"Wait. I want to hear what happened. From Angus. Come on. It's why we came. Please, Hadley? It'll be okay. What can he do to us?"

Hadley could think of several things, none of which she wanted to dwell on at the moment. But once again, she felt herself being pulled along by Josh's excitement.

"All right," she said. "Just leave the door open so we can make a quick getaway if we have to."

They walked through the door, into the gloomy house.

"And shut the door!" shouted Angus.

Josh looked at Hadley and shrugged. Hadley rolled her eyes. Together they headed in the direction of Angus's voice. At first they didn't see him sitting on the sofa, the room was so dark. He waved at the floor, which they took to mean that that was where they were supposed to sit.

When they were seated, Angus began, "If you're

smart, you'll listen to what I say. There's things that happen in this world that can't be explained. Things that would make your blood run cold. What goes on up there on that hill you'd be better off never knowing about. So I'll tell you what happened to my friend, Clarence Cuthbert, some forty years ago. And if that's not enough to keep you away from Hogback Hill, then you're stupider than I think you are."

Angus fixed Josh, then Hadley, with an appraising look before he continued. "Now Clarence, as I say, was my friend. So I told him what I'm telling you. Stay away from that place. No good can come of going up there. But Clarence was stubborn and foolish and he didn't listen to me. He'd heard my warnings, but he didn't believe. He was looking for excitement, adventure. The fool." Here Angus stopped and fixed Josh with his fierce gaze. Josh squirmed uncomfortably.

Angus snorted in disgust and continued. "So one morning I woke up to a peculiar sound out there," said Angus, nodding toward the front door where Hadley and Josh had entered. "A yowling sound, like nothing I'd ever heard on this earth, and the like of which I hope never to hear again. I went to the door and there, on the porch, was the most pathetic, most peculiar-looking creature I'd ever seen. At first I thought I must have still been sleeping. But gradually it dawned on me. What I saw was real. I was looking at Clarence. But he wasn't himself, not hardly. He was half man"— Angus leaned forward and spit the last words at Josh and Hadley—"and half cat! Black cat!"

29

Josh jumped and Hadley did too, even though she had known what was coming.

"Wow," said Josh, when he'd recovered. "Half cat! What did he look like?"

"Unnatural," said Angus. "A walking, screeching nightmare, right there on my porch. He was about your size—squirty for a boy, but big for a cat, if you see what I mean. I figure something went wrong with the spell, or whatever that creature up there uses to do her evil deeds. And there was Clarence, covered with black hair—fur I guess you'd call it—with cat's paws for hands and feet, and a tail. He had pointed furry ears and whiskers—but his face, his face looked just like Clarence. And that face looked at me with horror in its eyes. Horror! Damnedest thing I ever saw, and not a sight I'm likely to forget as long as I live."

"What happened to him?" Josh asked, looking dazed.

"I let him stay, once I got over the shock. He hung around a few days, eating cat food and drinking coffee out of a saucer, and staring at me with that look of horror on his face, like he'd seen the very devil or worse. But he didn't last long. The whole thing was unnatural, like I said. He died, and I buried him right there in the backyard." Angus leaned forward again, grinning dementedly at Josh. "Care to see the grave?"

Josh stood up, and so did Hadley. They began backing toward the door. Angus followed them, his eyes glittering. "There's things that go on up there that would make your blood run cold, boy, cold as ice. Cold as death. So if you're smart, boy, and I hope you are, you'll listen to Angus Tull like the rest of the kids around here. Stay away from Hogback Hill!"

By that time, Hadley and Josh had reached the door, opened it, and were walking quickly down the stairs. Hadley forgot about the missing step. Her leg fell through the hole and she tripped, sprawling on the matted grass in Angus's front yard. "Hadley!" Josh cried, turning to help her up. "Come on!"

"Stay away!" Angus called. "Or you'll be sorry."

Hadley and Josh ran, still hanging on to each other's arms, until they were out of sight of Angus's house and had turned the corner onto Hadley's street.

She and Josh stood looking at each other. Suddenly they both burst into hysterical laughter.

"You should have seen your face when he asked you if you wanted to see the grave!" Hadley said when she was able to talk.

"My face! What about your face when you fell through the step and Angus was right behind you!" Josh giggled. "I thought you were a goner."

Hadley's face grew sober. "You know, I never saw him act quite that way before. It was almost like he knows you want to go up there, Josh, and he was giving you a special warning." She shuddered. "You'd never get *me* up there," she said. "Not after that."

Josh was quiet. Then he looked at his watch. "Oh, no! I've got to go!" he said. "It's a quarter of six, and I told Mom I'd be home at five-thirty. She'll be wondering where I am. Hadley, meet me at the corner by

Larsen's store tomorrow morning and we'll walk to school together, okay?"

"Okay!" agreed Hadley. "See you later."

"I've got a plan!" Josh called as he ran toward home.

"Oh, great," Hadley called back. "I can't wait to hear it."

And she turned to walk to her house, where no one would be home wondering where she was.

6 Hadley let herself into the house and found a note from her mother:

Hadley, sweetie, thanks for letting me sleep. I guess I needed it. But be sure to wake me up tomorrow morning. How does French toast sound?

Love, Mom

Rummaging in the cupboard, Hadley came up with a can of chili-beef soup, and decided that would do for dinner. She warmed it up and ate it at the kitchen table, along with some crackers and a glass of milk. Her mother was always reminding her to be sure to have "something green" every night. She looked in the refrigerator, but everything that was supposed to be green looked sort of a sickly gray, or else was white with mold.

"Yuck."

She closed the vegetable bin and finished off her meal with some cookies and an apple.

After doing her homework, she got ready for bed and stood at her window. The night was cloudy, and she could barely see Hogback Hill. Good, she thought, getting into bed and opening her book. If I don't see it, maybe I won't think about it.

She must have been more tired than she thought, because she fell asleep with the light on, only to awaken with a start, her heart racing. She had dreamed again about the hag of Hogback Hill. It was the same dream as always: the twisted, deformed figure of the woman reaching out for Hadley, beckoning with bony fingers and calling, "Come. Come to me." But this time, Angus was in the dream, too, with the body of a cat and a cat's pointy ears and whiskers. "Stay away," he hissed. "Stay away from Hogback Hill!"

Hadley lay trembling for what seemed like hours, until her mother came home. Only when she heard the familiar sounds of her mother downstairs, hanging up her coat and opening the refrigerator for a snack, could she relax. She was almost asleep when her mother stepped into her room and softly kissed her good-night.

The next morning, Mrs. Patterson stood at the stove in her old blue bathrobe, her hair still tousled from sleeping, cooking French toast. She looked tired, as she always did lately, but still pretty.

"Mom," asked Hadley, "when you were my age, were you a foot taller than all the boys?"

"I don't think so," answered Mrs. Patterson. "I'm only five feet, two inches now."

"Did you have crooked teeth?"

"I never had to have braces, if that's what you mean," said her mother. "Why all the questions?"

"I just wondered if there was hope for me," said Hadley, "to end up looking like you."

"Why, Hadley," said her mother, surprised, "I must look a mess. But, honey, you look wonderful. You don't resemble me too much, with that dark hair and those green eyes. You look—well, like yourself."

"I guess I got more of Dad's looks," said Hadley.

"At least he left you *something*," said her mother. There was always a note of bitterness in her voice when she spoke of Hadley's father.

Hadley was sorry she had mentioned her father. She knew her mother didn't like to be reminded of him. Even though he had left them eight years ago, the mention of him still brought an angry frown to her mother's face. Mrs. Patterson claimed not to want to talk about him, not to miss him. But Hadley knew that when her mother stared for hours at nothing, her jaws clamped tightly together, she was thinking about him.

Hadley didn't know if her mother missed her father or was just angry, still, at the way he had up and left them, suddenly, without a word. To Hadley, his leaving seemed to have happened a long time ago. She couldn't really remember what it had been like to have him around. She tried to conjure up memories of him—what he did, how he spoke, even what he looked like—but the memories were blurry and insubstantial. What *she* missed was the way things used to be before her mother had so many worries and so much work.

"I met a new friend," Hadley said, to change the subject. "His name's Josh Carter. You know, his dad's the dentist who said I have buck teeth."

"He didn't say that," said Mrs. Patterson, flipping the French toast.

"Well, that's what he meant," said Hadley. "Anyway, I went over to Josh's house to play, and they invited me to stay and eat. It was fun. Mrs. Carter asked if we could both come for dinner this Saturday night, but I said you had to work. You don't think you could get the night off, do you?" she asked wistfully.

"What?" asked Mrs. Patterson absentmindedly as she searched for the syrup. "Get the night off? No, Hadley, you know better than that."

"Just asking," said Hadley, but she had known what her mother would say. Even if she weren't working, she'd have found some excuse not to go to the Carters' house for dinner. Hadley knew she wasn't the most popular kid in town, but at least she had had one good friend, Alison, and now it looked as if she and Josh were beginning to be friends. But Mrs. Patterson didn't know anyone, and she made no effort to meet anybody. Neighbors had stopped over when Hadley and her mother had first come to Possum Hollow, soon after her father had left. They had tried to be friendly, but in the face of Mrs. Patterson's continual rebuffs, they'd stopped calling.

On television, single moms were always dating, bringing home new boyfriends who drove their kids crazy. But Hadley's mother hadn't had one date, hadn't brought anybody home. She'd spent time at home with Hadley and she'd worked. And now, it seemed, she just worked.

"In fact," her mother continued as she put two pieces of French toast on a plate and handed it to Hadley, "I have to work extra this week. Tonight the Sheldrake is having a big Halloween party. A masked ball. We're expecting over two hundred people, and the place will be a madhouse. And Shirley, who covers for me on my day off, is sick, and who knows when she'll be back, so I won't be around much for a few days. Which reminds me, I'll have to get groceries before I leave for work today, and call the plumber about fixing this kitchen sink. If he can come today, and promises not to charge an arm and a leg, can you come right home after school to let him in?"

Hadley nodded, finishing her breakfast. She went upstairs to brush her teeth as her mother picked up the phone to dial the plumber. When she came back downstairs with her schoolbooks, her mother was on the phone.

"All right. Three-thirty will be fine. My daughter, Hadley, will be here to let you in. . . ." She raised her eyebrows questioningly to Hadley.

Hadley nodded and kissed her mother on the cheek, mouthing the words, "I've got to go."

"Now, if it's going to cost any more than that, you be sure to call me at work and check with me. . . . Yes. . . . Yes, the Sheldrake, that's right . . ." her mother was saying. Hadley walked out the door and closed it gently behind her.

7 Josh was waiting at the corner when Hadley got there.

"Hi," she called. "What's this big plan of yours?"

Josh got right to the point. "We're going trick-or-treating together tonight," he said.

"Great," said Hadley.

"On Hogback Hill," Josh said, looking expectantly at Hadley.

"What!" Hadley couldn't believe what she was hearing.

"Yes! Trick-or-treating on Hogback Hill! It's perfect!" Josh continued.

"That's what you said about going to see Angus," said Hadley.

"And it *was* perfect, Hadley. He was just like you said, only weirder. And the way I figure it, either Angus is totally crazy, or something strange really is going on up there. I want to find out which."

"I don't," said Hadley.

"Hadley, come on. It'll be a great—"

"Adventure. I know."

"Come on, Hadley. Please?"

"Oh, no, you don't, Josh," said Hadley. "You talked me into going to see Angus, but you're not going to talk me into this."

"But, Hadley, what about the light?" coaxed Josh. "Aren't you curious?"

"Yes," Hadley admitted. "I've been curious about that light for a long time."

"Well, there's only one way to find out what it is, and that's to go up there," declared Josh.

"I'm more scared than curious, Josh, and if you had any brains, you would be, too," Hadley retorted.

Josh's face took on a stubborn look. "Okay, then, I'll just have to go by myself," he said.

"You can't do that!" said Hadley.

"I'll have to," replied Josh, "if you won't come. And when my poor body, half boy and half cat, is found, you'll be very sorry."

"Josh, that's not funny!"

Josh merely shrugged.

Hadley tried another tactic. "You have to take Simon trick-or-treating," she said. "He said something about us all going together tonight."

"I already took care of that," said Josh. "I told my mom you and I would rather go by ourselves, and she said she'd take Simon out while Dad answers the door at home. She's so glad I have somebody to go with, I was pretty sure she'd say yes."

"Oh," said Hadley.

They walked along in silence. Hadley thought about

what Josh had said. He was right—she *was* curious. For years the hunchbacked woman had haunted her dreams. How many nights had she looked up at Hogback Hill, wondering about its secrets? How many nights had she awakened, like the night before, with the clammy sweat of her nightmares sending shivers through her? Maybe if she knew the truth, the nightmares would stop. Maybe if she went up Hogback Hill with Josh, she wouldn't have to be afraid anymore.

"All right," she said quietly. "I'll go."

8 The plan was for Hadley to dress in her costume and go over to Josh's house. They would leave from there to go trick-or-treating. They just wouldn't mention *where*.

Hadley waited for the plumber, who didn't show up until four-thirty, and watched while he fixed the sink. Then she tried on her wizard costume from the year before and was dismayed to find that it was much too short, and that it barely fit over her shoulders. Darn! She'd forgotten how much she had grown in just one year. Looking through her mother's closet, she found a long skirt with an elastic waist. She put it on and rolled the waistband over a few times. Then she tied a shawl around her shoulders and a kerchief around her head. For a final touch, she got some big hoop earrings from her mother's jewelry box and put them on.

Looking at herself in the mirror, Hadley thought, How original—a gypsy. But what difference did it make? No one was going to see her except for Josh's family. And the hag of Hogback Hill, she thought nervously.

Just for fun, she took an eyebrow pencil from her

mother's makeup case and colored one of her front teeth black. Hadley grinned at herself in the mirror. Great! Then, thinking that Josh's father would appreciate the effect, she darkened several more teeth.

She fixed herself a quick peanut-butter-and-jelly sandwich, grabbed a flashlight, and headed for the Carters' house.

Simon met her at the door, dancing with excitement in his little skeleton suit, the bones glowing slightly green as he stepped from the lighted doorway out into the darkness of the porch. Hadley was ready for him.

"Why don't skeletons go to scary movies?" she asked.

"Don't know!" said Simon gleefully, eagerly anticipating the answer to a new riddle.

"They haven't got the guts!" said Hadley.

Simon ran into the house, calling, "Mom! Dad! Why don't skeletons have the guts?"

Hadley laughed. She had looked up several more riddles, but it seemed Simon had enough to get mixed up for one night. "Josh?" she called up the stairs.

But instead of Josh, a tall skinny woman with long blond hair, thick black eyelashes, very red lips, a pink-and-white polka-dot dress, and pink high heels came lurching unsteadily down the hallway toward Hadley. In a peculiar voice that sounded a little bit like Josh's imitation of his teacher, the woman said, "Hadley, darling, you look simply divine. I'll have to borrow your earrings sometime. They would look smashing with my new hairdo. Care for a toothbrush, my dear?"

"Dr. Carter!" Hadley giggled. Then, grinning up at him to show her "missing" teeth, she said, "Sorry. Too late. Got no more teeth to brush."

Dr. Carter's large hands fluttered to his face in mock despair as Josh came down the stairs, looking terrific in his tight-fitting black costume with bones sewn all over, front and back, in all the right places. Josh looked at his father. "Dad, are you really going to wear that?"

"Why, Josh, darling, it's my very newest frock, flown all the way from Paris for this evening. You don't like it?" answered Dr. Carter, pouting his lipsticked mouth.

Josh rolled his eyes. "Let's get out of this crazy house," Josh said to Hadley as Simon came running into the room.

"Josh! Why don't skeletons have enough guts?"

"Bye, Dad," said Josh quickly, grabbing Hadley's arm and pulling her out the door. "Bye, Mom!" he called down the hallway. "Thanks for taking Simon."

"Remember, Josh, home by eight," said Josh's father, slipping back into his normal voice.

"Okay, Dad. See you."

"Whew!" said Josh when they were walking down the dark street. "We got out safely. I was afraid something would go wrong at the last minute and we'd get stuck with Simon."

"That was the easy part," Hadley said. "*Now* we have to climb up Hogback Hill."

9 There was no path to the top of Hogback Hill, and the underbrush was thick and tangled on the lower slopes. Branches pulled at their hair and snapped in their faces. Wild grapevines reached out to trip them, and pricker bushes snagged at their clothing.

Hadley's skirt kept tripping her, and the stretchy material of Josh's skeleton costume was getting caught on everything. "My mom's going to kill me when she sees what I'm doing to this costume," Josh complained. "Stupid bushes!"

As he flailed noisily about, trying to free himself, all Hadley could see were the bones, glowing with an eerie green light, dancing bizarrely in the blackness. Josh's flashlight beam jumped crazily through the sky.

"Josh! Turn off your flashlight if you're going to shine it all around like that," she called softly. "Anybody up there would see us coming for sure."

Hadley stood still, peering intently into the sudden darkness, waiting for her eyes to adjust. Looking back over her shoulder she saw the moon rising, huge and orange, over the town of Possum Hollow. She could see the swaying flashlight beams of the trick-or-treaters in the streets far below, and occasionally a laugh or a shriek carried up the hillside to where they stood. But there were no sounds on Hogback Hill, except for the wind moaning through the trees.

As she waited for Josh to get untangled and catch up to her, Hadley tucked her skirt up out of the way. Her eyes had begun to adjust to the darkness. Soon she could see a few feet ahead, but she couldn't help wondering what lay in all the dark places beyond her circle of vision.

Then the howling began.

Aaaarrroooooo.

The sound seemed to start at the base of her spine. It traveled right up to the back of her neck, making all the little hairs stand on end. It seemed to stop her heart on the way, by making it impossible to breathe.

"Josh?"

"Hadley?"

It started again, closer this time.

Aaaarrroooooo.

Josh came crashing through the bushes and grabbed Hadley's arm.

"What the heck *is* that?" he asked shakily.

"Coyotes," she managed to answer when she could find her voice. She had heard them hundreds of times before from her bedroom, but it was different, being right there in the darkness with them.

"Don't worry, they eat much smaller stuff than people," she told Josh. "Usually."

They stood for a moment, looking at the dim outlines of each other's faces.

"Come on," said Josh finally. "We can't quit now."

As the bushes and trees began to thin out, they could see to the very top of the hill. There, flickering faintly, was the light.

"Look!" Hadley said excitedly, pointing to the light.

Josh nodded, staring upward.

Soon the slope became steeper and more rocky, and the bushes gave way to an occasional stunted tree. The branches looked like groping, bony arms, and Hadley stayed away from them. She kept her eyes on the light. Sometimes it seemed to be beckoning them forward. The next moment, it seemed to warn them away.

Stepping carefully, sometimes using their hands to help them keep their footing on the steep gravel hillside, they climbed on until the roofline of a small cabin became visible. Josh nudged Hadley excitedly, and she nodded to let him know that she, too, saw it. Neither of them spoke as they inched closer to the building. A light shone from the window.

Another light, closer to the ground, glimmered with a warm, orange glow. Hadley caught her breath in surprise. It was a jack-o'-lantern.

The pumpkin grinned lopsidedly, its wide, unblinking eyes seeming to look right at them. The candle inside it suddenly fluttered in the wind, and the light caught on a pair of yellow eyes by the door, then another pair, then another and another, until they saw dozens of staring yellow eyes.

"Black cats," Hadley whispered breathlessly.

Something else caught her attention. On the ground next to the pumpkin was a bowl. Josh remained hidden in the shadows while Hadley took several steps closer. Inside the bowl were Halloween treats: Three Musketeers bars. She couldn't believe her eyes. Forgetting every warning she'd ever heard about taking candy from strangers, she reached into the bowl.

All at once the door flew open and a figure stood silhouetted against the doorway.

The figure had no head.

Hadley screamed.

Josh shouted, "Hadley, look out!"

Cats leaped into the air, yowling and screeching. Hadley stood for a moment, frozen, staring at the figure, who also stood motionless. Cats brushed past Hadley's legs, but still she stood, unable to move. Finally, she turned around and began to run after Josh, tripping, falling, crashing, rolling down the hill, heedless of the grasping branches and scratching thorns, her breath tearing from her throat in ragged sobs until at last she and Josh stood, breathless and exhausted, on the sidewalk that led from the foot of Hogback Hill to safety.

Josh had forgotten to bring his atomizer, and Hadley had a new fear as she watched him sitting on the sidewalk, wheezing and gasping for air.

"Josh," she said desperately, "are you all right? Should I get somebody?"

Josh shook his head as he continued his struggle to

breathe. He held up a finger, signaling Hadley to wait a minute. After what seemed like a very long time, his breathing became easier and more regular. Hadley tore her gaze from Josh's face and looked quickly behind her. No one was following them. Hogback Hill loomed, silent and seemingly empty, at their backs.

Josh stood up. "Let's get out of here," he said.

"Come on—we'll go to my house," suggested Hadley.

"Wait. What's your mother going to say when she sees us? We're a mess," said Josh. "She'll know we weren't trick-or-treating."

"It's okay; she's not home. Come on!" urged Hadley, eager to be gone.

They hurried down the block and around the corner to Hadley's house and let themselves in. When Hadley snapped on the light, they looked at each other and gasped. Josh's skeleton costume was torn in several places, giving the effect of broken and shattered bones, and the fabric was pulled and snagged. His face was scratched and bleeding slightly, as were his hands. Hadley glanced in the hall mirror and saw that she looked just as bad.

"My parents are going to kill me." Josh moaned when he saw himself.

"We can try to fix it," said Hadley. She didn't sound very hopeful.

But Josh was already thinking of other things. "Hadley," he said, his voice low and his eyes wide, "did you see what I saw?"

"What did you see?" asked Hadley carefully.

"It's what I *didn't* see," said Josh. His face looked pale and his voice was shaky. "That person didn't have a *head*."

"That's what I thought at first, too," said Hadley slowly. "But she did, Josh."

"She?" repeated Josh, bewildered.

"When she first came to the door, all I could see was her outline against the lighted doorway, and it looked like she didn't have a head. But then, by the light of the jack-o'-lantern, I could see that she *did* have a head, Josh, only she's so bent over it hangs down low, like this." Hadley hunched her back, held her shoulders forward and stuck her head out in front so that it seemed to grow out of her chest. "And with her long hair hanging down over her shoulders and around her face, it looked like just a body standing there. I was so scared I turned and started to run, but before I turned I saw her face."

"Wait," said Josh incredulously. "Are you trying to tell me there's a woman up there and she really *is* a hunchback, after all?"

"Yes," answered Hadley. Her voice sounded quiet and strange to her.

"And you saw her face? What was it like?" asked Josh.

"I—it's hard to describe," said Hadley. "She looked scared."

"*She* looked scared!" burst out Josh.

Hadley paused, searching for the right word to use. "Yes. Scared—and *shy*."

"Shy?" asked Josh. He shook his head in disbelief. "What was in the bowl?"

"You won't believe this," said Hadley. "Treats. Halloween treats. Like she was *expecting* us."

"What kind of treats? Salamander eyes or something?"

"No," answered Hadley softly, opening her hand. "Three Musketeers." They both stared at the squashed candy bar lying in Hadley's outstretched palm, the wrapper torn almost all the way off. "I took it from the bowl before I ran. It was still in my hand when we got to the bottom of the hill."

Josh was looking amazed, and Hadley couldn't blame him. She could scarcely believe it herself.

"Did she do anything? Like try to cast a spell on you?" asked Josh.

Hadley shook her head. "She just—stood there."

"Have you ever seen her before?" asked Josh.

"No."

"That makes it even stranger," mused Josh.

"Why?" asked Hadley.

"Well, this town's so small, everybody knows everybody, right?"

Hadley nodded.

"So if you've never seen her before, she must never come down to town."

Hadley nodded again.

"So where did she get the Three Musketeers bars?"

"I thought of that, too, Josh," she said. "She must come down from there."

They stared at each other in silence.

At the same time, they asked, "But when?"

After Josh left, Hadley stared for a long time at Hogback Hill. The light no longer shone. The hill was shrouded in darkness. A few stray clouds passed between its peak and the full Halloween moon. It looked deserted, desolate.

One of Hadley's questions had been answered. The hag of Hogback Hill was real! But who was she? And what was she doing up there? Hadley felt no closer to the answers than before, and more curious than ever.

10 The next morning, Josh was waiting for Hadley at the corner, looking dejected.

"What's the matter?" she asked.

"I'm in a lot of trouble because of last night," he mumbled. "My parents wanted to know what I'd been doing to get all scratched up like that. My mom wanted to know how I'd wrecked my costume. They wanted to know why I didn't have any candy."

"What did you tell them?" asked Hadley.

"The truth," said Josh. "That we went up Hogback Hill."

"Did you tell them why?"

"I just told them we wondered what it was like up there, which is true. I said we wanted to explore it because it's such a spooky place. They know how I like mysteries and stuff, so they weren't surprised, but they were mad. They said it was dangerous, and I should have told them where I was going. Mom got all upset about me climbing up there without my atomizer. They said I have to spend this weekend at home 'under supervision.' In jail, in other words," he finished miserably. "What did your mom say?"

"She didn't see me last night. She had to work late 'cause the Sheldrake had a big Halloween ball. So she slept in this morning," Hadley answered.

"You're lucky," said Josh. "My parents are always around, wanting to know every little thing I do. You can do whatever you want."

Hadley laughed. For the first time, she could see some advantages to her situation.

"Anyway, Hadley," Josh continued, "I've been thinking."

"Me, too," said Hadley. "I couldn't get to sleep last night."

"Me neither. And you know what? I don't think whoever is up there comes to town at all. I think someone must take her stuff, like the candy bars. Because even if she only came down once a month, or even once a year, people would have seen her. She'd have to go to stores to buy things. And then everybody would know about her; people would talk about her. People besides Angus, I mean. I've lived here long enough to know that. My mom says you can't sneeze around here without half a dozen people saying gesundheit!"

Josh was right. In Possum Hollow, everybody pretty much knew everybody else's business. People who kept to themselves, like Hadley's mother, were left alone. But that didn't mean people didn't talk about them. If the woman on the hill came to town, people would talk, sure as the sun came up every morning.

"So," Hadley said slowly, "the question is, who? Who visits her?"

"Maybe it's someone from out of town," suggested Josh.

"I don't know," said Hadley, thinking. "If a stranger kept coming to town to go up Hogback Hill, someone would have noticed. I think it's got to be someone from Possum Hollow. Someone who can come and go and walk down the street and shop in the store without anyone paying attention. Someone we see all the time. Someone normal."

"Normal?" Josh repeated.

"You know what I mean," Hadley said. "It's got to be someone we wouldn't suspect."

"Okay. So how do we find out?" Josh asked.

"I knew you'd say that," Hadley answered, grinning at Josh. It was funny. A few days ago, before she knew Josh, she'd have wanted nothing to do with such schemes. She had wondered what was happening on Hogback Hill, but she'd never thought she could find out. When Josh wanted to know something, there was no stopping him. And now here she was, thinking just like him.

"I already figured that out," she said with satisfaction. "We'll ask the Larsens who's been buying Three Musketeers bars lately!"

Josh looked incredulous. "Do you really think someone in a store is going to remember who bought a certain kind of candy?"

"It's not as dumb as it sounds, Josh," answered Hadley. "This is Possum Hollow, remember? Mr. and Mrs. Larsen know everything. It's worth a try—unless you have a better idea, that is."

"Okay," agreed Josh. "We'll go right after school."

11 As soon as school let out, Hadley and Josh walked down Sycamore Street to Larsen's Market. Old Mr. Larsen was sitting, as usual, behind the cash register, while Mrs. Larsen bustled about at the butcher's counter, cutting and weighing chicken legs for Mrs. Josie Sloan.

"Good afternoon, children," she sang out.

"Hi, Mrs. Larsen," they called back. Then, turning to Mr. Larsen, who was more than a little deaf, they shouted, "HELLO, MR. LARSEN."

"Hello there, Hadley, and what's the new feller's name? Oh, yes, John."

"It's Josh," corrected Josh.

"Yes, hello, John. How are you? Your mother was in earlier. You'll be having pork chops tonight, if I'm not mistaken, with potatoes, gravy, and green beans."

Hadley couldn't resist looking smugly at Josh. "What did I tell you?" she whispered.

"What can I do for you children today?" asked Mr. Larsen.

Hadley smiled and said, "Well, Mr. Larsen, this is probably going to sound kind of odd, but we were wondering who has been buying Three Musketeers bars lately."

"What, child? Speak up now."

Hadley looked around, embarrassed. Josh looked the other way, suddenly appearing to be fascinated by a display of headache remedies several aisles away. Seeing that he was going to be of no help, Hadley plunged on, more loudly this time. "HAS ANYONE BEEN BUYING THREE MUSKETEERS BARS LATELY?"

"Heavens, child, it was just Halloween. Sold lots of candy. Bags and bags of it."

"BUT HOW ABOUT THREE MUSKETEERS?" asked Hadley, feeling extremely foolish.

Mr. Larsen appeared to be thinking it over. There was a long pause, during which Hadley looked at Josh. He was looking down the aisle in front of him. With an expression of panic, he turned toward Hadley and put his finger frantically to his lips.

She looked at him, perplexed.

He drew his finger across his neck, pointed to Mr. Larsen, put his finger to his lips again as if he were trying to shush someone, and pointed to Mr. Larsen again.

What on earth is wrong with him? Hadley wondered.

Meanwhile, Mr. Larsen was talking again. "Well, now, it seems to me maybe Evelyn Dorsey bought some, though I couldn't be absolutely certain. It could have been Milky Ways; they're on the same shelf over there. . . ."

Hadley looked at Josh again. Mrs. Dorsey was his

teacher! But Josh wasn't paying any attention. He was still staring down the aisle, looking as if he were going to burst.

"And I believe Bud and Helen Fancett picked up some for trick or treat. I recall they had something of a discussion about it. . . ." Mr. Larsen paused again, lost in concentration.

Hadley looked at Josh. His eyes were practically bugging out of his head. What was going on?

Mr. Larsen resumed his recollections. "Of course, Angus buys 'em regular."

Angus! Hadley looked over at Josh again to see if he'd heard. Josh was looking positively ill.

She was about to say something to him when she saw the reason for his strange behavior. Her stomach gave a sickening lurch as Angus Tull stepped into view from behind the shelves of canned vegetables.

"Yep, Angus buys Three Musketeers regular," Mr. Larsen continued, oblivious. "Them and the Junior Mints, you know." Then, noticing Angus, he said, "Well, well, speak of the devil, and doesn't he just show up. Hello, Angus."

Angus didn't reply. He stood, glowering at Josh and Hadley with a murderous look.

"These two youngsters were just asking—"

"Nosy, interfering little brats," interrupted Angus. "I ought to teach you a lesson—"

Angus looked truly frightening. His face was very red, his blue eyes were blazing, his bristly white eyebrows were quivering, and his voice sounded peculiar, as if he were having trouble getting the words out.

"Take it easy, Angus," said Mr. Larsen. "Getting all riled up can't be good for that heart of yours. The children were only asking—"

"I don't care what they were asking." Angus looked at Josh long and hard, then turned his fierce blue eyes on Hadley and kept them there. "Mind your own business!"

He left his shopping cart containing the few items he had picked up and stalked to the door. He stopped by Josh, pointed his finger at Josh's chest, and said furiously, "And stay away from that hill!" Then he stormed out of the store.

Mr. Larsen looked from Hadley to Josh, his face puzzled. "Now what was that all about?"

Hadley kept quiet, trying to stop her trembling, letting Josh do the talking for a while.

"Uh, I—I don't know," Josh stammered. "He was acting pretty crazy."

"What's all this about Three Musketeers?" Mr. Larsen probed.

"We're doing kind of an investigation," explained Josh.

"You sure make a good eyewitness," added Hadley.

"Might have lost my hearing, but I haven't lost my mind," replied Mr. Larsen slyly.

"That's for sure, sir," Josh said as he and Hadley headed for the door. "Thanks," they both called, slipping away before Mr. Larsen could ask any more questions.

Out on the street they looked anxiously in both directions, but there was no sign of Angus.

"Do you think he knows we went up there?" asked Josh.

"I don't know," answered Hadley. "Do you think he heard me asking about the Three Musketeers bars?"

"Everybody in the whole store must have heard you," said Josh.

"Well, you weren't being much help!" answered Hadley. "Maybe he was still mad from the other day," she went on. "Or maybe he was mad because we were talking about him just when he came near."

"I can't believe he's been buying Three Musketeers bars!" Josh said excitedly. But then he shook his head, looking perplexed. "But Angus is the *last* person who'd be going up Hogback Hill with candy bars! He's afraid he'll get turned into a black cat like his friend Clarence."

"Yeah," said Hadley slowly, "you're right."

"So," Josh continued, "what about our other suspects?"

"Your teacher and the Fancetts," said Hadley. "Do you think Mrs. Dorsey is taking candy bars up Hogback Hill?"

Josh burst out laughing. Mrs. Dorsey was quite stout. "Can you imagine her getting up that steep part near the top?" he asked. "I don't think so. Anyway, she has an alibi, in a way. She gave out Three Musketeers bars at our class Halloween party. And besides, she's always at school."

"Yeah," said Hadley. "And the Fancetts are so old. Mr. Fancett walks with a cane, and Mrs. Fancett hardly ever comes out of the house."

"Angus is no spring chicken, either," Josh said.

"So you don't think any of our suspects are the one?" asked Hadley.

"We could stake out their houses," suggested Josh, but he didn't sound too thrilled about the prospect.

That gave Hadley an idea. "You know, Josh," she said, "we don't have to stake out their houses. We can stake out the foot of Hogback Hill."

"Yeah!" said Josh enthusiastically. "Sooner or later, we'll catch 'em red-handed."

"So do you want to go tomorrow after school?" asked Hadley.

"Yes!" said Josh. Then he frowned. "Tomorrow'll be my only chance. I have to stay home all weekend. Jeez! I wish my mother worked all the time like yours."

Hadley didn't answer. They'd been walking as they talked and had reached the Carters' driveway. "Okay, see you tomorrow then," said Hadley.

"Meet you at the corner in the morning?" asked Josh.

"Sure," Hadley answered, smiling.

She walked the nine-and-a-half blocks to her house. When she came to the street where Angus lived, she glanced nervously about, but there was no sign of him. She hurried the rest of the way home and locked the door behind her.

12 The next morning, Hadley and her mother sat at the kitchen table. Hadley was eating a bowl of cereal, and Mrs. Patterson was drinking coffee, trying to wake up.

"Shirley's feeling better and said she would come in for me on Sunday," Mrs. Patterson was saying. "So if I can just make it through today and Saturday, I'll finally have a day off on a weekend. What would you like to do?"

Hadley thought for a moment. "We could rake the leaves in the yard!"

"Sounds good," said Mrs. Patterson, smiling tiredly. "We have a million chores to get done, and raking the yard is one of them. I wish we could afford to hire somebody to do it."

"Maybe Josh could come over to help," said Hadley. Then she remembered that Josh was supposed to stay home that weekend.

Before she could say anything, her mother was answering. "Maybe, but we have a lot of other things to do as well, and I'm looking forward to a little time to just relax."

"Okay, Mom," said Hadley. There was no point in arguing, since Josh couldn't come anyway.

"That reminds me," said Mrs. Patterson. "I have to make another appointment for you with your friend Josh's father."

"You should come with me sometime and meet him, Mom. He's really nice. You should have seen him on Halloween night. He was—"

Mrs. Patterson interrupted her. "You're seeing a lot of this Josh fellow, aren't you?"

"Yes," answered Hadley happily.

"Be careful now, Hadley," said her mother. "Go easy."

"What do you mean?" asked Hadley, feeling confused.

"I just mean that if you get too attached to this Josh, you might be sorry. Remember how sad you felt when Alison moved away?"

"But Josh isn't going anywhere," said Hadley. "He just moved here."

"Yes, I know that. Honey, look, all I'm saying is that if you let people get too close, it can be hard on you if they leave."

Hadley didn't know what to say. "Don't you want me to be friends with Josh?" she asked.

Mrs. Patterson sighed. "Yes. I want you to be friends. I just don't want to see you hurt." She seemed about to say more, then shook her head as if she were shaking thoughts away. "Don't pay any attention to me. I'm just gloomy today, I guess." She shrugged, giving a weak laugh.

"Mom, I'd better get going. I'm supposed to meet Josh at the corner," Hadley said. She gave her mother a kiss.

"Okay, sweetie. Have a good day."

"You, too, Mom," said Hadley as she ran out the door.

She looked back to see her mother staring into her coffee cup, her mouth tightly set. Hadley didn't have to guess what she was thinking about.

13 That afternoon, Hadley and Josh sneaked around Angus Tull's house and took up a position on the lower slope of Hogback Hill. They made themselves comfortable—and, they hoped, invisible—on the soft bed of fallen needles under one of the stunted pine trees. They sat very still and tried to be quiet, but it was frustrating not to be able to talk to each other. At first they thought they heard all sorts of sinister sounds. Every twig that snapped, every leaf that blew, made them turn, expecting to see a furtive figure making its way past them up the hill. But after a while, they began to relax.

Josh whispered, "I always thought it would be exciting to be a policeman or a private eye. But stakeouts have got to be the most boring duty ever!"

Hadley wasn't bored. She was enjoying being with Josh, even though none of their suspects had appeared. Also, she noticed that the hillside was coming alive now that she and Josh had been still for some time. Squirrels scampered about, hiding nuts; birds landed in the branches of the pine tree, tilting their heads at her as if wondering what peculiar kind of bird she was. Ants went trooping by on their own mysterious, miniature business, while spiders waited patiently by their webs.

"Look!" she said. Her heart was pounding with excitement, and she almost made the mistake of moving to point.

Two deer had appeared on the hillside below them, munching on the tender lower branches of the bushes. Suddenly they lifted their heads, sniffed the air, and were gone, their white tails flashing like two white handkerchiefs.

"Deer!" cried Josh, laughing with relief. "You almost gave me a heart attack! I thought you saw . . ." He paused, turning slowly toward Hadley. Then he pounced on her, shouting, "Angus Tull!"

Hadley shrieked as they rolled down the hill a few feet. "Josh, we're supposed to be quiet!" she said when she was able to stop laughing.

"Come on, Hadley," said Josh, pushing himself up from the ground. "We might as well face facts. We're not going to see anybody today, and I'm freezing. Let's go."

They brushed the pine needles from their clothes and started down the hill. They were very quiet as they approached the bottom and, skirting well around Angus's house, stepped out onto the sidewalk.

"Well, that wasn't very thrilling," Josh commented. "What are we going to do next?"

"Do you really have to stay around home all weekend?" Hadley asked.

"Yeah," replied Josh dejectedly.

"I'll probably come back here tomorrow and give it another try," said Hadley. "It's Saturday, and if you have to stay home, I won't have anything else to do."

"Your mom has to work?" asked Josh.

Hadley nodded.

"You get to do whatever you want all weekend?" he asked.

Hadley shrugged. "Yeah. Well, Mom has Sunday off, and we'll probably do chores. But I won't see much of her before then."

"Lucky," said Josh. "Meanwhile, I'll be home getting riddled to death by Simon. By Monday I'll be a raving maniac. I'll be dying to go back to school!"

When they reached Hadley's house, Josh said he'd try to call Hadley over the weekend to see how her stakeout went on Saturday, and they made plans to meet at the corner on Monday morning.

"You're not afraid to do the stakeout alone?" asked Josh.

Hadley shook her head. She truly wasn't. She didn't really believe she was going to see the hag's mysterious visitor, and she had enjoyed sitting peacefully on the hillside, watching the birds and animals and insects. Besides, she didn't have anything else to do.

"Okay. Call me if you crack the case," said Josh with a grin.

"Which I probably will," replied Hadley, returning the smile. "See you. Oh, wait—here's a riddle for Simon. Maybe if you spend all weekend working on it with him, he'll get it right. What does a witch order in a hotel?"

"What?" asked Josh.

"Broom service," answered Hadley.

Josh groaned. "It's awful. He'll love it."

"Bye." Hadley waved as Josh walked down the street. "See you Monday."

14 Hadley woke up early Saturday morning, filled with eagerness to return to Hogback Hill. Her mother had left her a note on the kitchen counter.

Hadley, honey, I'm beat. I had to work until 1:30, so I'll probably sleep late. I have to be back at work by noon and won't be home until quite late. But we'll have all of Sunday together. There's sliced turkey for sandwiches or to heat up with gravy tonight.

Love, Mom

Hadley ate some cereal, then made a peanut-butter-and-jelly sandwich and put it into a paper sack along with an apple, some crackers, and a carton of juice. Next she got the binoculars and an old army blanket, and put everything in her backpack. When she was ready, she wrote a note underneath her mother's:

Dear Mom,
   I ate breakfast and made lunch, too.

She couldn't think of what else to say. It seemed that she and her mother did most of their communicating by note these days. Since it was too complicated to try to explain where she was going, she just added:

See you tomorrow. Don't work too hard!

Love, Hadley

She stepped out into the cool November morning and headed for Hogback Hill. It was only six-thirty, and the sky was just beginning to show a faint light in the east. She felt brave and adventurous and strangely excited, walking through the empty streets of Possum Hollow while everyone else was still sleeping. The town looked different at that hour of the morning, mysterious and otherworldly. She sneaked past Angus's house, but there was no sign of life.

She came to the spot where she and Josh had started climbing the hill the day before. She almost started up at the same place, when she had an idea. Continuing past the point at which the sidewalk ended, she proceeded to the farthest outreaches of town, an area where nobody lived. On her left there was an ugly pile of broken-down cars, rusty washing machines, and junk of all kinds in what used to be the Possum Hollow dump.

Hadley began looking carefully at the slope of the hill. The undergrowth was as thick and tangled on this part of the hill as it was elsewhere. It seemed to be an impenetrable barrier of thorny branches and made Hadley think about the prince trying to chop his way through walls of briers to reach the Sleeping Beauty. Then she thought of Rapunzel, with her long, long hair, locked away high in a tower in the deep, dark forest. Maybe the hag is under a spell, too, Hadley thought, and I'm the only one who can break it. She shook her head, laughing at herself.

Then she saw it. There was a small opening in the thick wall of brush. Looking around and seeing no one, she slipped through the opening and discovered, as she had hoped, that there was a path that led up the hill. It wasn't much—just a narrow place where the undergrowth had been tramped down and the branches pushed back enough to allow a person to slip through without too much struggle.

She had found the path that the hag's mysterious visitor used; she was sure of it! The back of her neck prickled with excitement as she began following the trail upward. When she came to where the trees began to grow thin and sparse, she stopped and hid herself in a clump of small pine trees away from the well-traveled route. She spread out the army blanket on a patch of ground from which she'd be able to clearly see both the path and the outline of the cabin.

She began to wait. Taking the binoculars from the pack, Hadley pointed them at the hag's little house and peered intently at the windows, the door, the yard. There was no sign of movement. Then she remained very still, and, once again, the small creatures who inhabited the hillside grew accustomed to her presence and went about their business.

As time passed with no sign of another human being, Hadley's mind began to wander. She thought about Josh, at home with Simon for the entire week-end, and she smiled. She thought about her mother, · home sleeping off the exhaustion of work so that she could go back and work another twelve- or thirteen-hour day. Mom might as well live up here on Hogback Hill, Hadley mused, for all the fun she ever has. The thought made her feel uneasy, but the truth was that her mother's behavior puzzled Hadley. She didn't want her life to be like her mother's and she wondered if there was anything she could do about it.

Hadley wondered, too, about the strange remarks her mother had made at the breakfast table the morn-ing before. Her mother *had* been gloomy. It wasn't fair to think Josh was like Hadley's father or anybody else. Josh was just Josh. And Hadley liked him, no matter what her mother said.

By late afternoon Hadley's food was all gone and she had wrapped herself up in the army blanket to keep away the creeping chill. The shadows of the pine trees were disappearing into the falling darkness, and Hadley decided that it was time to go home.

She was gathering up her things and stuffing them into her backpack when she became aware of a steady shuffling on the hillside below her. Standing straight and absolutely still, she stared at the place where the path entered the clearing. Closer and closer came the scuffling footsteps, along with the sounds of crunching leaves and breaking twigs. It sounded so loud that she thought she would see not a person, but some huge creature emerging from the trees.

71

But when a figure stepped into view, it was a person, all right. Even in the gathering gloom of twilight, there was no mistaking who it was. Stopping for a moment to catch his breath was Angus Tull.

15 Hadley stared, terrified, praying that her hiding place was good enough. Angus Tull!

She wished Josh was with her. She wished she and Josh had talked about what they would do if they actually saw the hag's visitor. Josh had said Angus was the last person who would be climbing Hogback Hill, but here he was. Watching him struggling to catch his breath, Hadley realized that Angus was a very old man. What brought him, with a pack on his back, clutching his chest and gasping for air, to the top of Hogback Hill?

She stood, immobile, trying to decide what to do. She knew what Josh would do. He would follow Angus the rest of the way up the hill and see if he could find out what was going on. Hadley didn't like to think what Angus would do if he caught her on Hogback Hill.

Angus collected himself and walked the rest of the way to the cabin, knocked, and went inside. Several black cats followed him through the door. Hadley waited a moment, took a deep breath, and began creeping silently toward the house.

The windows were closed against the November cold, but the door had bounced open a crack after Angus went inside. Hadley stole right up to the door, flattened herself against the wooden boards, and strained to hear the voices coming from inside.

". . . all I know. I'm getting too old to get up this blasted hill, carrying all this stuff." It was Angus's voice.

"I don't need so much, Angus," answered another voice, softer but somehow similar. "And you really don't have to come so often."

"That's not the point, Netta, and you know it," replied Angus, his voice quarrelsome and impatient. "What if something happened to me? Where would that leave you?"

There was a long silence. Netta! So that was her name! A cat and two kittens began rubbing against Hadley's legs, and she hoped they wouldn't start screeching, as they had before.

Then Netta said quietly, "Someone knows about me."

Hadley jumped.

Angus shouted, "What?"

"Someone knows I'm here," repeated Netta.

"What are you talking about?" said Angus furiously.

"A girl. And someone else. They came on Halloween night."

Hadley's heart was hammering against her chest.

"Did they bother you?" Angus's voice rose angrily. "Those nosy, interfering brats! Did they—"

"No, no," Netta said hastily. "Nothing like that. I frightened them, actually. They ran away."

"Damn kids," muttered Angus. "I know who they are. I warned them to keep away from here when they came snooping around asking questions."

"This girl . . . she seemed different. She had a kind face. I wished—"

Angus interrupted. "Children aren't kind, Netta. They're cruel. You remember what happened before."

Again there was a silence. Then Netta said softly, "I remember."

"Now, Netta, those brats coming here only proves my point. It's no good anymore. We can't have you staying here. Those kids probably told half the town about you by now. They'll all be trooping up here to torment you. Why, I'll worry to death about you. Netta, it's time. There's an opening at the nursing home, and I want you to take it."

"No, Angus. You must try to understand. I can't go there. I'm used to it here. The peace, the quiet, my cats, the wild creatures. I can do as I like. You might not think that's much, but it's what I'm used to. I won't go where I'll be closed up and told what I can do and when I can do it. I'd die there."

"Netta, you're being melodramatic and you know it. They'll take care of you. You'll get medical attention. Don't you try to tell me you're not in pain."

"My back's no worse than it's been for a long time, Angus. I can stand it. What I can't stand is the idea of leaving here. I don't need to be taken care of. I won't do it, Angus. I won't speak of it anymore."

There was a sound that Hadley was quite sure was Angus's fist pounding on a table. His voice was exasperated when he said, "Netta, I'm trying to make you see reason. We can't go on like this any longer. Don't you understand? I'm only trying to do what's best for you!"

There was another sound, like a snort. Netta answered quietly, "What's best for me, Angus? Or what's best for you?"

There was no answer.

"It was convenient for you to have me come here fifty-seven years ago, and now it's convenient for you to have me go down. But I've learned to like it here, Angus. If you really want to do what's best for me, you'll find a way for me to stay here."

No one spoke for a long time. Finally, Angus said in a tired voice, "All right, Netta, you win. But how can I rest easy when my sister's up here all alone, depending on me, and me eighty-one years old? Someday this old carcass of mine just plain won't make it up this hill. Then what'll you do?"

"We'll think of something, Angus. We always have, haven't we? Now, you'd better get along before it gets any darker."

"I'm going to break my fool neck one of these nights," Angus grumbled. Hadley heard the sound of a chair being pushed back. She wanted to keep listening, but it sounded as if Angus would be coming through the door at any moment, and the last thing she wanted was to be discovered eavesdropping by Angus Tull. She hid in the bushes and waited until Angus disappeared down the path.

Her brain was whirling. The hag—Netta—was Angus's sister! Fifty-seven years she had spent on top of Hogback Hill! Hadley couldn't imagine it. Why, she thought, Netta must have been a young woman when she came here.

Slowly making her way down the hill through the darkness, Hadley knew that she would return to Hogback Hill. She wants me to come, Hadley thought. She said my face was kind.

16 As soon as Hadley got home, she called Josh.
"Josh? Hi, it's Hadley."
"Hi," answered Josh. "How'd the stake-out go?"

"You won't believe this!" Hadley said. "I found a path, the one that the hag's visitor uses all the time. So I followed it, and hid near the top of the hill and waited and, just as I was about to give up and go home, I heard somebody coming. You'll never guess who it was!"

"Who?" asked Josh.

"Guess," said Hadley.

"Who was it? Come on," said Josh eagerly, "just *tell* me!"

"All right," said Hadley. "It was"—she paused for dramatic effect—"Angus Tull."

"Angus! What was he doing up there?" cried Josh excitedly.

"He was bringing Netta groceries."

"Netta?" asked Josh hesitantly.

"That's her name!" said Hadley. "She has a name. Netta Tull."

"Netta *Tull?*"

"She's Angus's sister," said Hadley. "And here's the really unbelievable part—she's been up there fifty-seven years!"

"Wow," Josh said softly. "Fifty-seven years." They were both quiet for a moment. "Why?"

"I don't know," answered Hadley. "He wants her to leave and go to some home, but she doesn't want to. She told him we'd been there."

"She did? What did he say?"

"He was really mad. Called us interfering little brats. He said we would tell everyone and the whole town would be going up there to torment her. He said children are cruel. 'Remember what happened before?' he asked. But, Josh, I don't care what Angus says; I want to go back."

"He'll really be on the lookout for us now," said Josh.

"Probably," said Hadley.

"How did you find all this out, anyway?" asked Josh.

"I sneaked up after Angus and hid outside the door. I could hear them talking inside," said Hadley.

"What if he'd caught you?" said Josh.

"I was a little worried about that, too," said Hadley.

"I wish I'd been there!" Josh cried.

"I was wishing the same thing when Angus first showed up!" Hadley joked.

"So when do you want to go back?" asked Josh.

"I'd really like to go tomorrow," said Hadley, "but it's my mom's day off, and we usually do something together. Plus, you have to stay home, right?"

"Yeah," said Josh gloomily. "Here you're tracking down dangerous suspects and I'm stuck watching cartoons with Simon."

Hadley laughed. Then she said seriously, "Josh? Don't tell anybody, okay? About Netta?"

"Okay. I mean, who am I going to tell—Simon?"

"Just don't tell anybody. Angus is so sure we will, I want to prove he's wrong. Besides, it sounded like— well, like something happened before, something to do with kids; I don't know. But until we find out, let's keep this a secret."

She thought the idea of a secret would appeal to Josh, and it did.

"My lips are sealed," he vowed. Then he added, "What was she like? Did she seem crazy?"

"No," said Hadley slowly. "She didn't act crazy at all. Actually, Angus sounded crazier than she did, at least from what I heard."

"I wonder what they're up to?"

"I don't know," said Hadley. "But I want to find out."

"Me, too!" said Josh.

"Do you want to go after school on Monday?" asked Hadley.

"Sure," said Josh.

"Okay. See you at the corner Monday morning?" asked Hadley.

"I'll be there," said Josh.

That evening, Hadley baked brownies with nuts inside and icing on the top. She put some on a plate so that her mother would see them when she got home. The rest she wrapped carefully in aluminum foil. She wanted to have something special to take to Netta on Monday.

As she stood at her window that night, looking up at the softly shining light, Hadley felt not fear, but a strange excitement. She felt a deep curiosity about the woman who lived on the hill and a conviction that, no matter what Angus said, Netta wanted her to come back. She thought of her dreams, of the woman crying, "Come to me, come to me."

"I'm coming, Netta," she said. "I'm coming."

17 The next morning, Hadley was up and about before her mother awoke. She mixed up pancake batter, set the table, and spread strips of bacon in the frying pan to cook. Her mother always got the coffeemaker ready the night before, and Hadley turned it on. It wasn't long before Mrs. Patterson appeared at the door to the kitchen, smiling sleepily.

"Dirty trick, Had," she said. "I might have been able to sleep through the smell of coffee *or* bacon, but never both."

"I figured I had to give you the double whammy to get you out of bed," said Hadley.

"Mmm," said her mother, pouring a cup of coffee and sitting at the table. "Now that you've got me up, what do I have to do next?"

"First you can relax and eat breakfast," said Hadley. "But—"

"I know—since you cooked, I have to clean up."

"Right," said Hadley with a grin. "It's only fair. Then we have to do all the usual boring stuff like changing the beds, doing the laundry, and getting groceries."

Her mother groaned. "I'm going back to bed."

"Wait—then we can rake the leaves. And then I was thinking we could go to the movies this afternoon," Hadley finished.

"I can see you've given this some thought," said Mrs. Patterson. "I just hope it's a good movie, or I'm liable to fall asleep. This past week has been awful."

It was on the tip of Hadley's tongue to suggest once again that her mother try to find a job that wasn't so exhausting, but at the last minute she said instead, "Mom, why would somebody—a young woman—hide away from the whole world and never see people or get married or go places or anything?"

Her mother put her coffee cup down carefully on the saucer and said, "What's this all about, Hadley?"

"I just—"

"Has someone been talking to you about me?" asked her mother.

"A-about *you*?" Hadley said, surprised. "No."

"Because if I don't want to get married again after what I went through the first time, it's perfectly understandable."

Hadley stared down at the bacon sizzling in the pan, feeling bewildered. She remembered sitting on Hogback Hill thinking that her mother might as well live there, too. Now, when she was asking about Netta, her mother thought she was talking about *her*.

She thought about what her mother had told her about her marriage to Hadley's father. She had been "madly in love" with him, she'd said. Hadley recalled the pictures in the old trunk in the attic. One, taken when her parents were both eighteen, was their wedding picture. Hadley's mother, her long hair piled on top of her head in an elaborate mass of curls and flowers, was holding the arm of a tall, skinny boy wearing a tuxedo that looked several sizes too large. Her mother's upswept hair and red lipstick made her look older than eighteen, but the boy on her arm didn't look much older than Hadley herself. Hadley had asked where all the other people were, and her mother had said sadly that no one was there. They had gone to a justice of the peace because her parents and his parents were all dead set against the marriage. "They said we were too young," Mrs. Patterson said with a sigh, "and of course they were right. But we didn't believe it then."

The rest of the story Hadley knew only too well. Her mother began working as a waitress, and her father kept getting jobs and losing them. Soon Hadley's mother was pregnant. Hadley remembered a picture of her father holding her, looking proud but unsure of himself. Finally, he had gotten a job at a lumber mill, but when hard times hit, Hadley's father, being one of the newest workers, was one of the first to be laid off. Hadley's mother had told Hadley how she had awakened one morning to find him gone without a word.

Mrs. Patterson's voice had a bitter, mocking edge when she spoke about him. "He could have taken another job, but he was too proud to take the jobs he could have had. Did he think waitressing was the most glamorous job in the world? He just plain couldn't face up to the responsibility of having a wife and a child, and when things got too tough, he ran away." Her mouth twisted defiantly. "And we've been just fine without him."

Hadley's mind returned to the present. As she lifted strips of bacon out of the pan and put them on a paper towel to drain, she tried to remember what her mother had just said. Something about having good reasons for not getting married again.

"I know, Mom," she said.

"No one has said anything to you about this?" asked her mother.

"Nobody, Mom, really," Hadley answered quickly. "I wasn't even talking about you. I was just—I was thinking about something else."

"Good," said Mrs. Patterson. "I know how people like to talk around here, and I . . . Well, it doesn't matter. I didn't mean to jump on you, honey."

"It's okay, Mom."

"When your father walked out on us, I promised myself I'd never let anyone do that to me again. We don't need anybody else. We're fine, just the two of us, aren't we?" There was a beseeching note in Mrs. Patterson's voice, and Hadley knew her mother wanted it to be true.

"Sure," Hadley answered uncomfortably. But she didn't really agree with her mother. Yes, they were fine, just the two of them. But it would be nice to have a dad like Josh's and a brother or sister. And it was fun having a friend—like Josh. Wasn't her mother lonely?

She piled the pancakes onto two plates, spread strips of bacon alongside, and carried the plates to the table. Then she poured two glasses of orange juice and sat down to eat.

"This looks wonderful, Had," said her mother, buttering her pancakes. "Maybe later you can read your social studies report out loud to me. Remember how I used to come home from waitressing and put my poor, tired old feet up on the coffee table while you read?" she asked, smiling fondly at Hadley. "That was fun, but I sure don't miss waitressing. No more swollen ankles for me."

Hadley smiled weakly at her mother. So that was that. She couldn't ask her mother to go back to a job she hated. She helped her mother carry the dishes to the sink, then went upstairs to strip the sheets off the beds.

Later that afternoon, as they sat together in the darkened theater waiting for the movie to start, Hadley thought about her mother and Netta Tull. That night, she awakened from a strange dream. In it, she climbed Hogback Hill and knocked on the door of Netta's cabin. A woman came to the door, but when Hadley looked up to see her face, it wasn't Netta, after all, but Hadley's mother.

18 After school on Monday, Hadley and Josh walked toward Hogback Hill, made sure the coast was clear, headed to the secret path, and started climbing.

"How did you ever find this path?" asked Josh.

"Simple deductive reasoning," said Hadley modestly. "Actually, I was trying to think like you do. Like a detective. I figured there had to be a path somewhere."

"It's a lot easier walking here, that's for sure," Josh commented. "And we won't get ripped to shreds like we did on Halloween."

"I was thinking," said Hadley, "that it seems kind of rude to suddenly appear at Netta's door out of the blue. She isn't used to visitors. I was thinking we should stand out in the clearing where she can see us, and let her decide what to do."

"Okay." Josh shrugged. "Sounds good to me."

They walked slowly into the open, where they would be clearly visible from the house. Several cats blinked sleepily at them from the steps.

Hadley pointed. "Look. They're not all black."

"So much for Angus's stories," Josh said.

The cats showed no interest in moving from their places on the sunny steps. Hadley and Josh stood uncertainly in the clearing, wondering what to do if Netta did not appear.

But then the door opened slowly, and there was Netta. She simply stood in the doorway, staring their way. Hadley nudged Josh and, haltingly, they walked closer. Netta continued to stare, her bright blue eyes, so much like Angus's, moving little by little over every inch of Hadley and Josh, seeming to find them fascinating. No one spoke, and Hadley began to feel very uncomfortable.

Finally Netta said, "You're the ones . . . who came before."

"Yes," Hadley answered, glad for the silence to be broken. "We came the other night. Halloween."

"What are your names?" asked Netta.

"I'm Hadley. Hadley Patterson."

"And I'm Josh Carter."

"Netta. Short for Henrietta," the woman said briskly. "Netta Tull."

"Pleased to meet you," Hadley and Josh said politely.

They stared at one another for several more moments, again without speaking. Hadley was surprised by her first good look at Netta. The woman *was* bent over, so much that she stood no higher than Josh's four feet, eight inches. Hadley stood about a head taller. And, as Hadley had tried to describe to Josh, Netta's back was hunched so that her head hung forward from her neck. The hump on her back looked, Hadley thought, just as if she had a football tucked under her dress in the back. Her long hair wasn't hanging free, as it had been on Halloween night, but was twisted into a neat bun at the back of her neck. She wore an old-fashioned–looking dress in a faded flower print and heavy black woolen stockings. What surprised Hadley was that the "horrible hag" wasn't horrible at all. Except for her hump, which Hadley was already growing used to, she appeared very much like other older women Hadley saw every day.

Still Netta stared, almost hungrily, as if she couldn't get enough of looking. Maybe if I hadn't laid eyes on another human being besides Angus for fifty-seven years, I'd stare, too, thought Hadley.

"W-we're sorry we ran away the other night," Hadley stammered. "It was the cats."

"They scared us to death when they started screeching," Josh added.

"You don't have to lie," said Netta brusquely. "I know what I look like."

Hadley didn't know what to say. "W-what do you mean?" she asked.

"I'm grotesque. Children are frightened of me. I know it quite well," Netta answered, her blue eyes flashing.

Hadley shook her head. She looked at Josh, not knowing how to explain. "No, it wasn't that," she said.

"We couldn't even see you, not really," said Josh.

"You're not—grotesque," said Hadley.

"We just had the jitters because of all the stories about you, and it was dark, and then the cats started screeching," Josh went on.

Netta gave him a sidelong glance. "What are the stories about me?"

Hadley's heart sank. Why had Josh said that? They couldn't tell Netta what people said about her.

"Come, come," urged Netta. "I know my brother has been telling stories to keep you children away. I've always wondered what he said. Did you know Angus is my brother?"

"Yes," Hadley answered. "I mean, no. Well, we guessed he was," she finished lamely.

Netta looked at Hadley slyly. "You guessed, eh? Well?"

"Well, what?" Hadley asked, feeling thoroughly confused.

"What are the stories about me? Come, child, tell me."

Hadley looked at Josh.

Josh began reluctantly. "They say—" He stopped.

Netta looked at them impatiently.

Hadley said as quickly as she could, "They say you turn people into black cats. They say you have a heart of stone." She stared down at the ground after this awful confession, wondering what Netta would do, and was surprised to hear her laugh. It was an odd sound, like dry leaves skittering over the sidewalk.

"A heart of stone, you say! Why, I never gave Angus credit for that much imagination." She laughed again.

"After all this time, I shouldn't wonder if it's true. Heart of stone. My, my."

Hadley continued staring at the ground, wishing they had never come.

"What were you thinking of, coming here after hearing such stories?" Netta asked.

Hadley could feel Netta's eyes staring intently. "I beg your pardon, ma'am?" she asked.

"Why did you come here? And please don't call me ma'am. I've told you my name."

"We came to find out who lived up here," Josh said.

"I can see the light from my bedroom window, and I knew someone must be here. I knew there was no such person as 'the horrible hag,' but—" She stopped, aghast, hoping that Netta hadn't heard.

But of course she had. "'The horrible hag'? Is that what they call me?" she asked.

"Yes, ma'— Yes, Netta," Hadley answered miserably, wishing more than ever that they had never set foot on Hogback Hill.

"Go on," prompted Netta. "You were curious? To see this hag?"

Josh shrugged. "I guess so. I mean, we just wanted to know the truth."

"Ah, the truth," commented Netta. Then, sharply, "And what brought you back?"

"Well, we knew that someone must visit you— because of the Three Musketeers bars," Josh replied.

"Oh, yes," said Netta, and to the children's surprise,

she grinned. "I put those out for Angus, as a sort of joke, I guess. I saw the flashlight beam and thought he was coming, though I couldn't imagine why, at that time of night. Of course, I never thought it would be the two of you. I suppose you realize you gave me quite a fright."

Hadley nodded.

"And then you wanted to know who was supplying me with candy bars, is that it?" Netta continued.

"Yes," replied Josh. "We did a stakeout at the bottom of the hill, but we didn't see anybody."

Hadley decided to tell the whole story and get it over with. "So I came back by myself. I waited down there"—she pointed down the hill—"in those trees, until Angus came. Then I followed him up here. I heard some of your conversation," she confessed. "And I decided to come back."

"Why?" asked Netta quietly. "Angus said you'd come to torment me."

"No!" cried Hadley. "I came because—I thought you sounded nice. Because you didn't seem anything like those old stories Angus told. Or anything like in my dreams."

Josh and Netta were both looking at her curiously. All at once she remembered the brownies.

"Here," she said, digging through her pack until she found the shiny package, which she handed to Netta. "I brought you these."

Netta took the package and opened it.

"I made them myself," Hadley added.

Netta's face got a funny kind of crumply look. "I was right about you," she said slowly. She turned and opened the door. "Won't you come in, Hadley Patterson and Josh Carter, and visit with me?"

19 Netta held the door as Hadley and Josh stepped into the cabin. Hadley hadn't given any thought to what the inside of the house might be like, but it was more wonderful than anything she could have imagined.

"It's like living in a tree house!" Josh exclaimed.

Netta looked pleased.

There were windows everywhere, so the sky filled the room in all directions. But what fascinated Hadley was the oddest and most beautiful furniture she had ever seen. The flat surfaces of the tables and chairs were made from narrow wooden boards, but the legs and arms were made from tree branches of all different sizes, with the bark still on them. Curved branches had been added for decoration, giving the furniture the look of graceful, living trees that just happened to be shaped like tables and chairs.

"It's like furniture elves would have," she said delightedly, "or fairies!"

Next to one of the large windows stood an easel and some paints and brushes. On the easel was a canvas. Hadley walked closer and saw that the painting was of the view from the window. It showed the town of

Possum Hollow, far below, looking like some distant otherworld.

There were paintings and books everywhere in the little room. Hundreds and hundreds of books filled the shelves, overflowed onto the tables, and spilled into piles in the corners. Every inch of the walls that wasn't taken by a window or a bookshelf was covered with a painting.

Immediately, Hadley recognized a portrait of Angus. There were other portraits, of people she didn't know, and paintings of all sorts of animals: Netta's cats, the wild birds, deer, rabbits, and coyotes who shared Hogback Hill with Netta.

Netta stood without speaking as Josh and Hadley looked around wonderingly. Hadley pointed to a portrait of a young man with Angus's bright blue eyes and the same determined set to his mouth. "Is that Angus? When he was young?" she asked.

"Yes," answered Netta. "Handsome, wasn't he?"

"And this is just the way he looks now," Josh said, pointing to a recent likeness.

"It shows that stubborn streak of his, doesn't it? Maybe that's why he doesn't care for it. Angus thinks my painting is silly. He says it's a waste of time." She laughed her short laugh. "But I tell him, if there's one thing I have, it's time. If it weren't for my books and paints, I'd probably be stark, raving mad." She stopped for a moment and added, "Maybe I am, at that."

Hadley smiled and shook her head, but she wished Netta wouldn't say such things.

95

"Who do you think this is?" she asked, pointing to a portrait of a lovely young woman.

Hadley and Josh stepped closer to get a better look.

"It's you, isn't it?" asked Josh.

"You were beautiful," said Hadley.

"Ha!" Netta snorted. "Oh, I wasn't hard to look at, I suppose, but that was before—" She broke off, brushed a strand of stray hair away from her face, and shook her head. There was a long moment when no one spoke. Then, turning back, Netta asked, "Shall we have those brownies now?"

Josh nodded eagerly.

"Sure," Hadley said.

Netta got some milk from an old ice chest. "Milk goes best with brownies, don't you think?"

Hadley and Josh nodded, and Netta poured them each a glass. Hadley noticed that there were only two chairs. She and Josh stood uncertainly, until Netta perched herself on top of the ice chest. She pointed to the chairs, saying, "I'm not equipped for company, as you can see."

While they ate, Netta continued to stare at them in a way that would have been rude if she had been anyone else. But Netta, unused to visitors as she was, seemed simply amazed to find herself sharing brownies with two eleven-year-old children.

Suddenly Netta said, "I suppose you find this all very peculiar."

"It's nice here," Hadley answered honestly. "But I wonder why, well, why you're here."

"For fifty-seven years," Josh added.

"That, children, is a very long story." Netta stood up and started clearing away the glasses and plates. "And you had better start home now, hadn't you? It gets dark so early these days. Did you find Angus's path?"

"Yes," said Hadley.

"Smart," Netta said approvingly.

They walked to the door and stopped. "Well," said Josh awkwardly, "good-bye."

"Good-bye, Josh Carter," said Netta.

"Good-bye, Netta," said Hadley.

"Thank you for the brownies," said Netta.

They stepped through the door and began walking away from the cabin. Hadley turned back and asked, "Would it be all right if we came back to see you? I mean, we won't—"

"If you don't want us to," finished Josh.

Netta's eyes searched their faces. "Would you really like to come back?" she asked.

Hadley and Josh looked at each other, then nodded. "Yes."

"You come anytime you want," Netta said. She laughed her dry laugh. "I'll be here."

"Uh . . . what about Angus?" asked Josh. "He won't like it very much, will he?"

"Don't you worry about Angus," replied Netta. "I'll take care of him."

Hadley and Josh smiled, imagining Netta giving Angus a scolding.

"You're not like the others, are you?" she asked suddenly.

"What?" asked Josh.

"What others?" echoed Hadley.

"No, you're not. I can see that. I wonder why Angus can't see that? Never mind. Be careful on that hill now."

"We will," promised Josh.

"Bye," called Hadley.

They started down the hill in the twilight. When they turned to look back, Netta stood framed in the doorway, as she had been the night that they first saw her, waving good-bye.

"She's nice!" Josh said.

"I know," said Hadley in a puzzled voice. "It makes the whole thing even stranger, don't you think? It would almost make sense if she was like Angus says she is. But she's not. I mean, she's a hunchback, but big deal. After a while, you don't even notice it."

"But she thinks she's"—What was the word?— "grotesque."

"I wonder why. And I'm curious about what she meant when she said she wasn't hard to look at, 'but that was *before*.' Before what?"

"Yeah," continued Josh, "and what about when she said you and I are different, not like the others? What others?"

"I want to find out," Hadley said fiercely, turning to Josh. "I want to know what happened before and who the others are and what the long story is. I want to know why a nice lady like Netta is up there all alone."

"Remember you heard Angus say something about how children are cruel?" asked Josh.

Hadley had been thinking about that, too. "Yeah. It makes me wonder what happened. . . ."

They left the secret path and walked until they reached the sidewalk. Looking about for signs of Angus, Hadley said, "Do you want to go back tomorrow?"

"I can't," said Josh. "I have a trumpet lesson at four."

"Oh," said Hadley. She felt anxious to see Netta again soon. "Would you care if I went without you?"

Josh thought for a minute. "No, I guess not," he answered. "But tell her why I couldn't come. I don't want her to think it's because I didn't like her—or thought she was grotesque."

Hadley smiled at Josh. "I'll tell her," she said.

20 The next day, when Hadley stepped into the clearing outside Netta's house, the door opened immediately. "You just missed Angus," Netta called. "Did you meet him on the path?"

"No," said Hadley.

"That's strange." Netta frowned. "He only left five minutes ago. In a bit of a black humor, I'm afraid."

"Because of Josh and me?" asked Hadley. "He doesn't like us very much."

"Angus doesn't like anything very much, Hadley," said Netta with a sigh. "The way he was carrying on, I wonder if he's taken leave of his senses. I can't seem to convince him that you mean me no harm. At his age, I don't like to see him get so agitated."

"He *is* pretty old," Hadley said.

"Yes. Old and tired. Tired of living, I do believe." Then her face brightened. "I'm very glad to see you," she said, smiling. "Where's your friend Josh?"

"He wanted me to tell you he'll come to see you soon, but he had a trumpet lesson today."

"Well, that's very important. Music and painting and reading are some of my greatest pleasures. I tell

Angus that's what he needs, something to do, something to take his mind off the past. He says I'm a fine one to talk, living here the way I do. But never mind all that. Won't you come in? It's gotten rather chilly, and I have a nice fire going."

They went into the little cabin. Netta put another log in the wood stove and asked, "Would you like some tea?"

"Yes, please," said Hadley.

"With honey?" asked Netta.

Hadley nodded. Then she found herself blurting, "Netta? Would you tell me the story? About why you're here?"

As soon as she had spoken, she felt herself blushing furiously. She was sure Netta would turn away, tell her to mind her own business, or say that she wouldn't understand.

But Netta just looked at Hadley for a long moment. Then she said, "Why?"

It was such a simple question, but Hadley didn't know how to answer it. How could she explain the way the light on Hogback Hill had seemed to shine, night after night, into her thoughts, how the image of the woman on the hill had wound through her dreams, how that woman had become tangled up in Hadley's mind with her mother? How could she explain that in some way she hoped that Netta's story would help her understand her own?

"Because I've wondered about you for so long," said Hadley, as honestly as she could.

Netta poured two cups of tea, added honey, and said, "Milk?"

Hadley nodded.

Netta moved slowly, taking her time preparing the tea. Finally, handing a cup to Hadley, she settled into the rocking chair across from the chair where Hadley sat. She blew thoughtfully at the tea to cool it. She was, Hadley thought, deciding how to start.

"You want to know why I came here, and why I've stayed all these years," she said. "I can see why you'd wonder. It's an unusual story, I suppose, to others, but to me . . . Well, it's just the way it is. It all began such a long time ago. . . ." She paused, and Hadley knew her mind was traveling back, remembering. Netta began haltingly, with long pauses between sentences.

"It was 1936. Angus was twenty-four then, and I was sixteen. Angus was about to be married to his sweetheart; Mary Eliza O'Toole was her name. Oh, Angus was full of beans, he was, back in those days. Handsome, wild, cocky as could be. He turned all the young ladies' heads. But Mary Eliza put an end to Angus's roguish ways, indeed she did. He took one look at that china-doll face of hers and fell head over heels in love. He'd only known her for a month when he asked her to marry him, and she agreed.

"Now, I was only sixteen, but I had my doubts about Mary Eliza from the first. When I looked into those big, blue, china-doll eyes, I felt I was looking into sparkling blue ice. Cold, she was. I didn't think for a minute that she cared for Angus the way he cared for her.

"Well, one day about two weeks before the wedding,

we packed a picnic lunch, and my mother and Angus and I—my father died in the First World War—went for a ride over to Rockybottom Creek. We had recently bought our first automobile, and Angus was always looking for excuses to drive it."

"I've been to Rockybottom Creek," Hadley said. "It's pretty there."

Netta seemed startled to hear Hadley speak, as if she had forgotten Hadley's presence in the rush of memories.

"It certainly was lovely that day," Netta continued. "It was one of the first warm days of spring, and the creek was running hard from the melted snow, and the birds were singing. We ate and we napped in the sun and then, inevitably, I guess, talk turned to the upcoming wedding.

"I've never been able to remember exactly how it started, but I think Mama asked Angus if there was any harm in waiting a little longer, until he and Mary Eliza knew each other better. I remember I thought that Mama was right, and that if some time went by, Angus would discover what we could see so plainly, that Mary Eliza didn't love him. I didn't want Angus to make a mistake, you see, and get hurt.

"But Angus didn't take it that way at all. He got himself all worked up about it. How dared we speak against Mary Eliza! He said she had warned him we would try to come between them. She had him all twisted up against us, you see. Maybe Mama shouldn't have said anything, but she spoke out of love and concern for her son. It's just that Angus was so blindly in love, he couldn't see anything but Mary Eliza and what she wanted him to see."

Hadley thought suddenly of her mother saying how she had been "madly in love" with Hadley's father. Hadley hoped she would never be "madly" in love. It seemed to make people do foolish things.

"The picnic was ruined, of course," Netta went on. "Angus was furious. You've seen that temper of his. He threw the blanket and picnic hamper into the car and called to us to get in; he was leaving. So we did. We felt awful. Mama was apologizing and trying to explain, but Angus was acting like a crazy man. He had that car going full speed down that twisty, muddy road. Mama and I were frightened to death and were crying out for him to slow down, when he lost control of the car on a curve and smashed into a tree."

There was a silence as the echo of the crash seemed to reverberate through the little house. Netta stared out the window, seeing, Hadley knew, not the sky outside but the events of that long-ago afternoon. Netta rose shakily and offered more tea to Hadley, but Hadley's was untouched; she'd been too absorbed in Netta's story to drink it.

Netta continued quietly. "Mama died. I had what the doctors called a compression fracture of the spine, but I didn't know that for a long, long time. For weeks I was out of my mind. They said I had a head injury, but part of it was that, deep down inside, I knew that something awful had happened, and I didn't want to wake up and face it.

"When I did come to my senses, I was in a great deal of pain. I was in my own bed at home, but it didn't feel like home anymore. Angus had married Mary Eliza after the accident, and it became clear to me right away that I was an unwelcome visitor in what was now their house.

"I slowly realized, too, that it was painful for Angus to have me around. He tried to hide it, of course, but he could scarcely bear to look at me. I was, and have been ever since, a reminder to him of what he did that day."

Netta's gaze traveled slowly from the window to rest on Hadley's face. "Oh, my," she said. "I'm sorry, dear. This isn't a very happy story."

"But why did you come up here?" asked Hadley.

"I had nowhere else to go," Netta answered simply.

"Why not?" said Hadley. "You could have lived lots of places."

"Oh, how to explain this to you?" wondered Netta. "You see this hump on my back, don't you?"

"Yes, but—"

"For some reason you're not horrified by it—or by me."

"No," answered Hadley. "Why should I be?"

"But the other children in town are frightened by the stories about me, aren't they? Frightened and disgusted?"

"But they don't know you!" Hadley protested.

"They've never seen you. They've just heard those awful stories." She felt a sudden surge of anger at Angus. What reason could he have for saying such things?

"And what do you suppose they would think of me if they did see me?" Netta persisted.

"But you're nothing like Angus says!" cried Hadley. "Why does he say such stupid things?"

"Let me tell you the rest of the story, and maybe you'll understand why I did what I did," Netta said. "As the months went by, my back grew worse and worse. The fractured bones in my spine tightened up more and more, and I began to grow stooped. It was painful, and I was trying to learn how to live with that. Now, before the accident, I'd had a beau—did I tell you that?"

Hadley shook her head.

"His name was Thomas. Oh, our romance wasn't serious, really, but we used to whisper about being married some day. One day when I was well enough, Thomas came to call. We went for a walk. Looking back, I see that Thomas acted quiet and strange when he saw me, but I was so glad to see him and to be up and about that I guess I didn't pay too much attention. A group of children began following us down the street. 'She's a hunchback!' they shouted. They followed along behind us, calling, 'Thomas loves a hunchback! Thomas loves a hunchback!'

"I was so humiliated. I ran to my room and hid there. Later, I overheard Mary Eliza talking to Angus.

She said, 'You see, Angus, the effect she has on people. She gives me the shivers. I don't know how much longer I can bear having her in the house.'"

"That's ridiculous!" Hadley broke in. "She was just being mean!"

"That's what I kept waiting for Angus to say, but he didn't. I looked in the mirror and saw myself as I imagined others saw me: misshapen, hideous, a horror. I knew Thomas would never be back. I compared myself to that perfect little china doll, and I knew that I would never be loved by anyone. I kept hearing those children's shouts, and I told myself I would never let that happen to me again.

"The next day I went to Angus and told him I wanted to go away somewhere, anywhere, where no one could ever ridicule me again. A part of me was waiting for Angus to tell me I was being silly, that I didn't look so bad, and that those children were just being children. But instead he looked at me and said that it would probably be best for everybody if I left. It was a way, you see, to keep peace with Mary Eliza.

"He was the one who suggested that I come here. Our parents had owned the land and built this cabin. All we had to do was fix it up a bit. . . ."

Netta stared down at the tea in her cup for a long time. "Angus told everyone I was going away to a hospital in Chicago. Later, he began making up stories to keep curious children away. And so, here I've been, for all these years. . . ."

Hadley struggled with her thoughts. She found herself filled with fury at Angus. "How could Angus do that to you? You must hate him. I hate him!"

Netta looked at Hadley with obvious surprise. "Hate him? No, I don't hate him. Angus's life hasn't been easy. He's had to live with himself and what he did. And Mary Eliza, I'm afraid, wasn't much consolation. He didn't have a moment's peace with her. As it turned out, she soon found someone a little more handsome and a little richer than Angus, and that was the end of that."

"But, Netta," said Hadley, "he let you think you were some kind of—monster. He wrecked your whole life."

"Hush, now, it's too late for all that," Netta said.

"But you don't have to live up here anymore. You could live with me and my mom," Hadley offered eagerly.

"That's kind of you, Hadley, but don't you see? I was the one who wanted to come here. I could have come down anytime I wanted to. I wasn't Angus's prisoner. But I've grown used to it here. It's my home. The birds and the deer and the coyotes, they accept me the way I am."

Netta fussed nervously with her hair for a moment, tucking loose strands into the bun at the back of her neck. Hadley could see that her suggestion that Netta leave Hogback Hill had made Netta uncomfortable.

"Is there anything you want me to do? Can I bring you anything when I come again?" Hadley asked gently.

"Thank you," Netta replied, "but I'm fine for now. Angus always leaves me with much more than I need. It's part of his guilt." She gave Hadley a conspiratorial grin. "Will you be coming back soon?" she asked. "And your friend Josh?"

"We'll come anytime you want," answered Hadley.

"Well, you and Josh have many things to do other than to visit an old lady like me," said Netta. "Come when you can. As I said, I'll be here."

"Okay," said Hadley. "Well, bye." She began walking to the door. Then, surprising herself, she turned back and kissed Netta softly on her weathered cheek. "Thank you," she said, "for telling me."

21 As Hadley stepped into the clearing, she zipped her jacket against the cold wind that was sweeping down Hogback Hill, making the bare branches of the trees rattle and the gray clouds scud across the darkening November sky. She heard the crunch of dried leaves and the snap of twigs under her feet, the pine boughs that sighed and rustled as she passed, and she noticed that the shadows were deepening all around her.

Then one of the shadows moved. Hadley stifled a scream as a dusky shape emerged from the darkness and stood before her in the path. She couldn't make out a face, just a glimmer of pale white hair and two white eyebrows. Angus!

Hadley stood motionless. She knew he saw her, had known she was coming, had been waiting for her to come down the path. Why did he just stand there, silent and threatening? Hadley remembered Netta's voice saying, "I wonder if he's taken leave of his senses." She pushed the thought away.

When Angus did speak, his voice sounded thick and strangled. "You," he growled, "keep away from here.

Stay off this hill. We don't want you. You or your friend."

Hadley swallowed. She found herself answering back, "Netta *does* want us."

"Leave her be!" Angus commanded. "You don't know what you're talking about. Damned brat!"

"Netta wants us to come see her," said Hadley. "She said so."

"No! She doesn't. She can't. She's different. Can't you see? Leave her be!" Angus shouted, his voice growing shrill and strained.

Hadley didn't want to talk to Angus anymore. And she didn't want to stand on the dark hillside with him any longer. She ducked her head and began to run as fast as she could. With her arms flailing, she pushed Angus aside, rushed past him, and went running down the path. Her heart was banging in her throat as she imagined Angus's footsteps behind her. She thought she could feel his breath on her neck even as she heard his curses fading far behind her. She ran and ran until she arrived, breathless, at her own front door. Fumbling for the key, she opened the door, slammed it shut, and stood panting on the other side.

As soon as she could breathe normally, she went to the phone and called Josh.

"He's crazy!" Josh said when she told him of her encounter with Angus. "He's nuts. A lunatic! Are you okay?"

"I guess so," Hadley answered. "But wait. There's more. Netta told me everything."

And Hadley told Josh Netta's story. When she had finished, Josh was quiet for a while. Then he said hotly, "It's all Angus's fault."

"I know," said Hadley.

"The accident was bad enough," Josh continued, "but afterward, when she wanted to go up there to live, he should have told her not to pay any attention to what those stupid kids said. They were just being jerks!"

"I know," said Hadley. "But he didn't. He was even worse than the kids. He made her go up there, and now she's so used to it, she might never come down."

"Yeah. Hey, does she really want us to go back?"

"Yes," Hadley answered. "Do you want to go tomorrow?"

"I can't," said Josh. "I have to finish my science project. How about the next day?"

"I have an appointment with your dad," said Hadley.

"Okay," said Josh. "We'll go Friday."

"Perfect!" said Hadley. "We have the day off, remember? Teacher conferences."

"All right!" exclaimed Josh happily.

22 When Hadley left Dr. Carter's office on Thursday afternoon, she wondered if she would ever be able to speak like a normal person again. Dr. Carter had shown her the wire he used along her top front teeth, so she knew that it was very thin, but it felt like a thick steel cable between her lip and her teeth. The piece of plastic that was molded against the roof of her mouth made her feel as if she had four pieces of bubble gum stuck up there. The contraption was, Dr. Carter had explained, a bite plate, which she would wear for several weeks before getting her braces. Braces! Hadley didn't think there was room in her mouth for anything else.

She was so busy exploring the bite plate with her tongue that she didn't hear Josh when he ran up behind her. "Josh!" she exclaimed, except it came out sounding kind of funny. "You scared me to death."

"What?" asked Josh. "Oh, I forgot. You got a bite plate. Never mind. You'll get used to it. But, Hadley, listen, did you hear? I can hardly believe it! Just when—"

"What are you talking about?" asked Hadley. "Did I hear what?" She stopped, feeling ridiculous, when she heard the way her words sounded. Maybe she wouldn't talk anymore until she got her braces off. How long did that take? Two years? Three?

But Josh seemed to have understood her well enough.

"About Angus. He's dead. He died this morning. I guess he had a heart attack. I just heard it at Larsen's."

"Angus is dead?" Hadley repeated stupidly. "He can't be dead."

"Well, he is," said Josh.

"I just saw him yesterday," Hadley said, as if that made it impossible for Angus to be dead. She felt a peculiar feeling in her stomach. She had never known anyone who had died.

"It's creepy, isn't it?" Josh went on. "After the way he ambushed you yesterday on the way home from Netta's?"

Hadley was still having trouble believing that Angus was dead, but when Josh's words sank in she suddenly cried, "Netta! Josh, what about Netta? What will she do? She doesn't know—how could she? We'll have to tell her. We'd better go now."

"Wait a second," said Josh. "It's already dark, Hadley. We can't go now. My mom won't let me, for one thing. There's no school tomorrow, remember? We can go first thing in the morning."

Hadley nodded, realizing the sense of what Josh was saying. Netta would be all right until morning. "But what will she do without Angus?" she said.

"Well," said Josh, "she's got us."

"Yes," said Hadley, "you're right. She's got us. But—"

"Look, I've got to go," said Josh. "Dinner was almost ready when I came to find you. I'll be over first thing in the morning, okay?"

"Okay," Hadley answered.

"And Hadley? You're talking better already," Josh called back over his shoulder.

Hadley smiled to herself. She had forgotten all about her bite plate.

On the way home, her tongue worried the roof of her mouth, and thoughts of Netta and Angus worried her mind. She didn't really feel sorry that Angus was dead. She hadn't known him well, and what she had known of him wasn't very nice. But what *would* Netta do now that Angus was dead? It was frightening to think that, except for her and Josh, no one in the world knew about Netta.

115

23 "What on earth?" Netta exclaimed when Hadley and Josh arrived at her door the next morning. "What are you two doing here? I've been out of touch, I know, but unless I'm mistaken, Friday is a school day."

"Parent-teacher conferences," Josh explained as he and Hadley followed Netta inside.

"Ah," said Netta. "Well, how lucky for me. May I offer you some tea?"

"No, thanks, Netta," said Hadley. She and Josh had decided it would be best to get right to the point. "We— Well, we came to tell you something."

"Something serious, by the looks on your faces," Netta said.

"Yes," Josh said. "It's about Angus."

"He died, Netta," said Hadley. "Yesterday morning."

Netta's hand went to her throat. "Was it his heart?" she asked quietly.

Hadley nodded.

Netta rose and began fussing with the teapot. "I always worried about his heart," she said. Then, as if to herself, she murmured, "Poor Angus. Maybe he's found some peace at last."

Hadley felt confused by Netta's calmness. She looked at Josh, and he shrugged.

"Aren't you sad?" she asked Netta.

"What?" said Netta. "Oh, yes. When I think of Angus, there's a lot to be sad about. But, remember, he was eighty-one years old. And he was tired. Tired of coming up here, tired of keeping our little secret. He wanted me to come down and enter some kind of home so he'd be relieved of the responsibility for me, but I wouldn't hear of it. He was simply tired of living his life, I believe. It wasn't a very happy one."

"You won't have to go to a home, will you?" asked Hadley. "They can't make you, can they?"

Josh added, "Because Hadley and I were talking about it, and we can help you now like Angus did. We can bring you whatever you need."

"And everything will be like before," Hadley said eagerly.

"No, children," said Netta gently. "I don't know what will happen now, but I do know that everything will not be like before. Things will change. They'll have to." She paused, staring blindly at the teapot. "And maybe that's good."

Hadley and Josh were silent. Netta turned to them and smiled briefly. "It was good of you to come," she said. "And I appreciate your offer of help. Right now I need some time to think. Some time to do my mourning for Angus. Some time to decide what to do next."

"Do you need any supplies?" Josh asked.

"No, thank you," answered Netta. "I'm fine for now. But would you be able to come back sometime soon?"

117

"We'll come whenever you say," Hadley offered.

"Would tomorrow be all right?" Netta asked.

"Sure," Josh said. "It's Saturday."

"We'll come," Hadley said.

"Thank you," said Netta as she sat down in the rocking chair.

Hadley and Josh said good-bye softly and crept out the door, leaving Netta rocking back and forth, staring out the window as if looking for her future there.

24 When Hadley got home that evening, there was a note from her mother.

Hadley, sweetie, hope your teeth are feeling better today. I'll see you tomorrow morning before I go to work. Good news—who says miracles never happen?—I have Sunday off again.

Love, Mom

The following morning, as Hadley and her mother ate breakfast, her mother asked, "Well, what are you going to do with yourself today?"

Hadley hardly knew where to begin. She hadn't had a chance to tell her mother anything about Netta, or Angus—or anything that had been happening ever since she and Josh had first become interested in Hogback Hill.

"Well," she said, "Josh and I have to go up Hogback Hill in a little while. He's coming over soon."

"Oh," said Mrs. Patterson. "I really should meet this friend Josh you've been spending so much time with. What are you two going to do on Hogback Hill? I thought none of you kids ever went up there. Didn't you tell me everyone thinks it's haunted or something?"

"It's kind of a long story," Hadley began and, taking a deep breath, she tried to tell her mother about Netta, about how she and Josh had discovered her, and about everything that had happened since.

When she finished, her mother looked utterly astonished. "Hadley," Mrs. Patterson said finally, "this makes me feel very peculiar. All this has been going on in your life, and I didn't know a thing about it."

Hadley wiggled uncomfortably in her chair. "Well," she ventured, "there never seemed to be time to tell you."

"I'm not sure I would have been happy if I *had* known about it," continued Mrs. Patterson. "But now— Well, Angus is dead, and Netta sounds perfectly harmless."

"She is," Hadley reassured her mother. "I can't believe I ever paid any attention to those stories about her."

"What do you think Netta will do now?" asked Mrs. Patterson thoughtfully.

"I don't know," answered Hadley. "She said she needed time to think. We told her we'd bring her stuff like Angus used to, if she wanted us to, so she can stay on Hogback Hill."

"Are you sure you want to do that?" asked Mrs. Patterson. "It would be an awfully big responsibility."

"We don't mind," said Hadley eagerly. "We really like her. And it's nice on Hogback Hill. You should see her little house, Mom."

"Maybe I will someday," said Mrs. Patterson. She was quiet for a moment. Then she asked softly, "It was Netta you were talking about the other day, wasn't it? When you asked me why someone would live the way she has."

Hadley nodded.

"And I assumed you were talking about me."

Hadley stared down at the table.

Mrs. Patterson made a sound like a laugh. "Maybe someday the kids will be making up stories about me. The horrible hag of Possum Hollow."

"Mom!" said Hadley.

"I'm sorry, Had. I shouldn't joke. It's just that I feel as if you've held a mirror up to my face. And I'm not sure I like what I see."

Hadley didn't know what to say. "Netta's nice, Mom. You'd like her."

"I'm sure I would," said Mrs. Patterson.

"Mom?" said Hadley.

"Yes, sweetie?"

Before Hadley could say anything else, there was a knock at the door. "That must be Josh," she said, getting up from the table.

She returned to the kitchen with Josh.

"Hello, Josh," said Mrs. Patterson.

"You're home!" Josh said. Then he blushed deeply, saying, "I mean, it's nice to meet you, Mrs. Patterson."

Hadley's mother laughed ruefully. "It's nice to meet you, too, Josh. It sounds like you and Hadley have been having a very exciting time."

"I told her about Netta," Hadley explained.

"I told my parents, too," said Josh. "They say it's okay if I take things to Netta, but they want to meet her. How are we going to work that?"

"We'll have to see what Netta says, I guess," said Hadley. "Maybe she wouldn't mind if they came up. You, too, Mom."

"We'll see," said Mrs. Patterson. "Right now I had better get ready for work."

Josh helped Hadley clean up the kitchen. Then they called good-bye to Hadley's mother and started up the now-familiar path to Netta's house.

25 When they reached the top of the hill, Netta came to the cabin door, paintbrush in hand. "Oh!" she said, "I had hoped to be further along before you came. Never mind. Come in, come in. You might as well see it now."

Hadley and Josh stepped into the cabin to see what Netta had been working on. Their eyes were immediately drawn to a half-finished portrait on the easel.

"It's us!" Josh cried delightedly.

"How did you do it?" Hadley asked with amazement. "I thought people had to sit for hours and hours for portraits. It looks just like us. And we weren't even here!"

Netta looked pleased. "Goodness," she said. "If I waited for someone to sit here for hours, I'd never paint a picture. I look closely at things and paint from my memory. Why, you didn't suppose the birds and the deer and the coyotes came and posed for me, did you?"

Hadley looked curiously at Netta. She had expected Netta to be quiet, perhaps even gloomy, but instead Netta seemed to be in high spirits.

"I always do my best thinking when I'm painting," Netta went on gaily.

"What have you been thinking about?" asked Josh.

"Oh, many, many things," said Netta. "I was up most of the night thinking. And yet I don't feel a bit tired. Would you like to hear what I've decided?"

"Yes," Hadley and Josh answered.

"Sit, sit," urged Netta. She had been waving the paintbrush about as she spoke, and she put it in a jar of mineral spirits before coming over to perch on the ice chest. But she was too excited to sit still, and soon she got up again, walking around the room as she spoke.

"Angus had a will, of course," she began. "He kept it with a lawyer in town, Henry Updyke. Do you know him?"

"I know who he is," said Hadley. "He's real old."

"Angus's age, yes. Well, I expect Henry is in something of a dither right now. He'll be needing to see me about Angus's estate, and I don't imagine old Henry is too keen on climbing up this hill. He's the only soul, other than the two of you, who knows I'm up here. So the first thing I shall have to do is go to see Henry."

"Go to see Henry?" Josh repeated.

"In town?" Hadley asked in astonishment.

"Yes," said Netta, plainly enjoying the effect of her words. "In town."

Hadley and Josh stared, dumbfounded, as she went on. "Now, I appreciate the two of you offering to come up here to bring me supplies. And what I would like to do, if you are still willing, is have you do just that during the summer months. For my plan, you see, is to live in Angus's house during the really cold months when firewood becomes such a difficult problem, and to live here the rest of the year. If, of course, there is still enough money from my parents' estate, and I am quite certain that there is."

Hadley and Josh sat in stunned silence, as Netta went to the dresser and began pulling clothing from the drawers. "I imagine we should be on our way soon, don't you? I'll just take enough things for a day or two, until I can see Henry and put things in order, and then I'll be back to close up for the winter. I have to think of how to move the cats. Well, never mind that for now. They'll be fine for one or two days."

Hadley stared at Josh in amazement. "Netta," she said, "I thought you wouldn't ever leave Hogback Hill."

"I thought so, too," Netta replied as she tucked her clothes into a small cloth bag. "But all that's changed now."

"Why don't you move to town for good?" asked Hadley.

It was Netta's turn to look astonished. "Because," she answered, "I like it here." She paused. "But it's different now. I'll live here when I care to, not because I feel I must. Not because I'm frightened."

For Hadley it was as if a spell had been broken. She remembered the morning she had imagined Netta as Rapunzel in her tower, or the Sleeping Beauty waiting to be awakened. "Once, before I knew you, I thought that you might be a fairy-tale princess under a spell," she told Netta shyly.

"I *was* under a spell," Netta said. "For fifty-seven years. . . ."

"But no prince came along to wake you up," Josh said, teasing.

"No," said Netta seriously. "It was you two who woke me."

Netta's words filled Hadley with pleasure. "Us?" she asked.

"Your coming changed everything," Netta said. "It made me think again, about things I hadn't thought of for years. I began wondering about Possum Hollow and what it's like now. I began thinking about people I knew who are still there, people like Ed and Emma Larsen. I began to ask myself what I was doing here. All of a sudden, what happened fifty-seven years ago began to seem very faraway and unimportant. This might sound silly, but I realized that the way I was living was just . . . *habit*. Angus and I kept playing our parts in a play that had no meaning anymore. But I couldn't see that until the two of you came, bringing . . . bringing me the world. And Angus's death made everything clearer. It's time for me to come down from Hogback Hill."

Netta disappeared behind the curtain that separated her bedroom from the rest of the cabin. Josh and Hadley stared at each other for a moment, grinning. Even though she wasn't sure she understood it,

Hadley felt proud that she had played a part in Netta's decision.

Netta reappeared. "Which dress do you think I should wear? I don't suppose either one is quite the current fashion in Possum Hollow."

"They're both nice," said Josh.

"Maybe the blue one," suggested Hadley.

"All right," agreed Netta, stepping behind the curtain again.

"Where do you want to go first when we get to town?" asked Hadley.

"To Larsen's Market to get some things. Then to Angus's house to get settled. I'll give Henry Updyke a call so he can stop fretting. I'm sure he's fretting, knowing Henry. And then, well, we'll just see."

"You haven't seen the house for a long time," Josh said, then stopped. Hadley knew he was wondering if Netta was prepared for the house that Josh had thought looked haunted.

"No," said Netta, "but I shouldn't be surprised to find a mess on my hands. Angus never was much of a housekeeper—or a handyman. I do all the maintenance of this place myself. So I expect I have some cleaning to do, at the very least."

At the very least is right, thought Hadley. "We'll help," she offered.

"Thank you," said Netta as she filled bowls with food for the cats and set them out on the doorstep. "There. This place should be fine for a couple of days, and so should the cats." She took a deep breath and said quietly, "I guess I'm ready." Picking up her cloth bag, she turned to Hadley and Josh. "Shall we go?"

Hadley thought, absurdly, that there ought to be a brass band playing, or a flourish of drums, or some kind of dramatic background music like in the movies, to add emphasis to such an important moment. But instead, she and Josh and Netta simply closed the door and began walking across the clearing. Hadley remembered how she had felt the night she and Josh had climbed *up* the hill for the first time, and tried to imagine how it must feel to Netta to be going down for the first time in so long.

Hadley and Josh each held one of Netta's elbows when they reached the steep, graveled part of the hillside.

"Goodness," exclaimed Netta. "I'm going to have to get some of those sneakers you two are wearing. These old shoes of mine are slippery."

They reached the bottom of the hill and walked past the dump. When it was time to leave the deserted sidewalk, Hadley could feel Netta's arm trembling in hers.

"Are you frightened?" she asked.

Netta considered this. "Yes," she said finally. "But that's all right. I'll get over it, I expect."

Hadley clasped Netta's elbow firmly, and they stepped out together onto the street. Netta peered anxiously ahead, squinting her eyes, trying to take everything in. A car passed by and Netta jumped away from the street, bumping Josh off the sidewalk. "So fast," she murmured apologetically.

As they turned onto East Street, a boy on a bicycle turned the corner, a sack of newspapers hanging from his shoulder. He rode up the sidewalk toward them, throwing papers onto the doorsteps. Hadley felt Netta stiffen beside her.

"Hi, Scott," said Hadley as the boy drew near.

"Hey, Hadley. Hey, Josh, how's it going?" said Scott as he flashed past. He turned around, started up the other side of the street, and, looking back, popped a wheelie.

Hadley laughed. "Show-off," she called.

"That looks very difficult," Netta said.

"It's not so hard," said Josh. Grinning, he added, "I could teach you in no time."

"That boy didn't pay me any mind," said Netta.

"Nope," said Hadley happily.

Hadley could feel Netta's grip on her arm begin to relax. Netta began looking about with interest and curiosity, asking questions about who lived in the houses they passed and exclaiming over how things had changed in fifty-seven years.

At Larsen's, Netta walked slowly down the aisles, putting some items into the cart and examining others with amazement. "Microwaveable. My, my," she murmured. When she reached the meat counter, she said softly, "Hello, Emma."

Emma Larsen turned from the beef she was trimming and looked questioningly at Netta. Her puzzled look changed to one of recognition, then doubt, then awe. "Netta?" she whispered. "My goodness, Henrietta Tull, is that really you?"

"Yes," answered Netta. "It really is."

"Why, I can scarcely believe my own eyes," said Mrs. Larsen, wiping her hands on her big white butcher's apron and coming around in front of the counter to embrace Netta.

"Ed, come see who's turned up after all these years!" she called excitedly toward the front of the store.

"What's that, Emma?" Mr. Larsen called back.

"I'll get him," said Josh, heading for the front of the store, where Mr. Larsen sat at the counter.

Hadley watched with interest as Netta and Mrs. Larsen and, finally, Mr. Larsen talked, the Larsens exclaiming over and over again at the remarkable fact of Netta's presence. From time to time, they stopped and simply stared at Netta, shaking their heads. "I suppose you've come for Angus's funeral," said Mr. Larsen.

"Yes," answered Netta, adding almost shyly, "I plan to be around quite a bit from now on."

"Well, that's just splendid," said Mr. Larsen, "just splendid. We're going to miss Angus around here, the ornery son of a gun, but it's good news to think you'll be with us now, Netta. Good news, indeed."

Hadley could see that Mrs. Larsen was bursting with curiosity. "Netta," she asked finally, "where *have* you kept yourself all these years? Angus spoke of a hospital in Chicago, but we could never get too much out of him. . . ."

"Emma, when I get settled, I'll have you over for tea and we'll catch up on all that," said Netta. "Right now

130

I've got to get to the house and see what's what, and give Henry Updyke a call to let him know I'm here."

"I'd like to see Henry's face when he hears your voice on the telephone!" Mr. Larsen laughed.

Josh and Hadley each carried a bag of groceries to Angus's—now Netta's—house. Hadley had been worried about what Netta would think when she saw the condition of the house, but Netta only said matter-of-factly, "Angus never did know how to take care of anything."

After Netta had put away her things and looked around a bit, she said, "Now you two should be on your way. I have calls to make, and you surely have better things to do on a Saturday than hang around this gloomy place. And I confess I'm feeling a bit tired from all the excitement. You come back tomorrow if you like, and see what kind of progress I've made cleaning this place up."

She refused their offers of help. Putting a hand on each of their shoulders, she said, "You've done enough. Now scoot."

As Hadley and Josh walked down the street, Josh said, "But we didn't do anything. Netta did it herself."

"She says we broke the spell," Hadley reminded him.

"I guess you're right," said Josh. He struck a heroic pose. "Just call me Prince Charming."

Hadley laughed. "Fat chance!"

26 The next morning was Sunday. Hadley rose early and was surprised to find her mother already in the kitchen, breaking eggs into a bowl, even though she hadn't come home from work until one that morning.

"Hi, Mom," said Hadley. "I was going to make *you* breakfast. What are you doing up so early?"

"Morning, sweetie. I didn't sleep very well last night. To tell the truth, I was up all night."

Hadley had been up most of the night, too, thinking about Netta—and her mother. During the night it had come to her that if something could happen as astonishing as Netta's leaving Hogback Hill, then maybe . . . maybe other things could change, too.

"Mom?"

"Yes, honey?"

"When Dad left, were you sad?"

Mrs. Patterson stared, surprised, at Hadley. "Yes," she said. Her face stiffened. "But angry, and hurt and humiliated, too. Why?"

"Do you *still* feel that way?" Hadley went on.

Her mother sighed, picked up her coffee cup, and

took a drink. "I try not to spend very much time thinking about how I feel."

"But do you?" Hadley persisted.

"Why are you asking me this, Hadley?"

"Netta came down from Hogback Hill yesterday," Hadley blurted. It wasn't really an answer to her mother's question, but it was all Hadley could think of to say.

Mrs. Patterson's eyebrows lifted in surprise. She waited for Hadley to continue.

"We—Josh and I—couldn't believe she'd do it. But she said that living up there, hiding from everybody, had just become a habit. She said that she'd been thinking, and all the things that happened fifty-seven years ago didn't seem to matter anymore."

"A habit?" murmured Mrs. Patterson.

"She was scared when we came down the hill. When we started to cross the road, I could feel her arm shaking, but she didn't want to go back."

Her mother didn't answer, seeming lost in her own thoughts.

"Mom?" Hadley said again as she moved closer to her mother and wrapped her arms around her.

"Yes, honey?"

"*Do* you still feel the way you did when Dad left?"

Mrs. Patterson was quiet for a while, thinking. "You know, Hadley," she said, "it's funny . . . I've spent all this time trying not to think or talk about your father and what happened between us. And now that you actually ask me how I feel about it, I find that I don't feel very much at all anymore. It was so long ago. I guess I'm not still mad, not really. I'm just sorry. Sorry it turned out this way, for your sake. And sorry for him. Because he'll never know what a great kid he has," she said fiercely, hugging Hadley to her.

Then she said, "You know, I couldn't sleep last night because I was thinking about your friend Netta."

"You were?" asked Hadley. It was her turn to be surprised.

"Yes. It made me uncomfortable to think that I was like her in some way. I didn't like it, but I didn't know what to do about it. Now you tell me what Netta has done, and"—her voice had grown very low, until it almost seemed that she was talking to herself—"maybe now it's my turn. . . ."

Hadley felt an odd excitement in the pit of her stomach. "What are you going to do?" she asked.

"I—I don't know," her mother replied. "That's the hard part."

"Get to know some people in town?" suggested Hadley.

"Like who?"

"I don't know. Like Josh's parents. Like somebody to go on a date with."

"A date!"

"Aren't you lonely, just working and coming home and working again? Don't you ever want to get married again?"

"What on earth?" exclaimed her mother.

"Everybody isn't like Dad, you know," said Hadley. "Josh's father is real nice."

Mrs. Patterson laughed and said, "You're not suggesting that I marry Josh's dad, are you? Wouldn't Josh's mother have something to say about that?"

"Mom! You know what I mean."

"I'm only teasing, Had. I guess I do know what you mean. But what happened with your father—I told myself I'd never let it happen again."

"Mom, you said yourself, it was a long time ago."

"Well, maybe it's hard for you to understand, but the very idea of going through that again scares me to death. What if it didn't work out?"

Hadley shrugged. "You'd be stuck with me, I guess," she said with a grin.

Mrs. Patterson smiled, looking at Hadley and shaking her head. "You know something," she said. "You went and grew up on me when I wasn't looking."

Hadley glanced hopefully at the mirror that hung by the kitchen door to see what her mother meant, but she didn't look any different. She was still too tall, with too many freckles and crooked teeth. She looked away with a shrug.

"Mom?"

"Yes?"

"How about getting a new job?"

"Why a new job?"

"Because I hate it when you're working all the time," said Hadley. "I don't like being here alone, eating alone, going to bed alone. It's no fun—and I'm scared at night."

As she said that, Hadley realized that it wasn't true anymore, not all of it. She wasn't scared at night, not since she had climbed Hogback Hill. Once she'd met Netta, the bad dreams had stopped.

But the rest was true. "I never get to see you," she said.

Mrs. Patterson got up from the table and started beating the eggs in the bowl nervously. "Goodness, Hadley, I'd have to think about that. The job I have pays better than anything I thought I could get."

She stopped suddenly, her hand holding the fork over the half-beaten eggs. "You'd really like it if I was around more?"

"Yes," said Hadley, and then she laughed.

"What's so funny?" asked her mother.

"Oh, I was just thinking about Josh. He'd think I was *nuts*," she said.

"Why?" asked her mother.

"He says he wishes his parents weren't home all the time so that he could do whatever he wants," Hadley explained. "But Josh doesn't always know what he's talking about."

27 Two weeks later, Hadley and Josh were walking home from Netta's house on a clear, cold November night. The moon was rising, gleaming and white, over the town of Possum Hollow. It shone on Hogback Hill, its light reflecting off the fresh snow, making the hill shimmer with a quiet, peaceful beauty. No other light shone at the top, for Netta's cabin was closed up tight, and she and her cats were settled into Angus's old house for the winter.

Josh and Hadley had been to Netta's to deliver an invitation to a trim-the-Christmas-tree party at the Pattersons' house. It had been Hadley's idea. Her mother had been reluctant at first, but was soon caught up in Hadley's enthusiasm. Netta was coming, of course, and Josh and Simon and their parents, and, Hadley reported excitedly to Josh, a man her mother knew from the Sheldrake.

"A man?" asked Josh. "Like a boyfriend?"

"I don't know," said Hadley. "He's a customer who eats there all the time. Mom says 'just a friend.'"

"That's what they always say," said Josh wisely.

Hadley laughed. "But, anyway, the best news is Mom told the owner of the Sheldrake yesterday that she was going to have to find a job with more normal hours. Mrs. McCleary—that's the owner—really likes Mom and doesn't want her to leave, so she and Mom are having a big powwow today. Mom didn't want to get her hopes up, but she thinks things might work out."

"That's good, huh?" said Josh.

"Yes," said Hadley. They walked along in silence for a moment. Then Hadley said, "Just think—if we hadn't decided to go up Hogback Hill on Halloween night, none of this would have happened."

"If *we* hadn't decided?" said Josh. "I seem to remember having to practically drag you up there."

"Okay, okay," said Hadley, "I admit it. But after that, things around here sure started to change."

"They sure did," agreed Josh. "But," he added ominously, "*some* things never change."

"Like what?" asked Hadley.

"Like Simon," Josh answered with disgust. "You want to hear his newest joke?"

"Sure." Hadley laughed.

"He says, 'Why did Netta cross the road?'"

"And what's the answer?" asked Hadley.

"'To get to the other side.'" Josh groaned.

"So what's wrong with that?" asked Hadley.

"So he finally gets the punchline right, but, as usual, the whole thing doesn't make any sense."

"I don't know about that," said Hadley.

Josh shook his head in exasperation.

Hadley laughed again. "In fact," she said softly, "it makes perfect sense to me."